# GREEN LUCK

# GREEN LUCK

•

## Gaby Pratt

*AVALON BOOKS*
NEW YORK

Published by Thomas Bouregy & Co., Inc.
160 Madison Avenue, New York, NY 10016


Library of Congress Cataloging-in-Publication Data

Pratt, Gaby.
  Green Luck / Gaby Pratt.
      p. cm.
  ISBN 978-0-8034-9985-0 (hardcover : acid-free paper)
1. Show horses—Fiction.   2. Show jumpers (Persons)—
Fiction.   3. Horse grooms—Fiction.   4. Show jumping—
Fiction.   I. Title.
  PS3616.R3835G74 2009
  813'.6—dc22

                                        2009024228




PRINTED IN THE UNITED STATES OF AMERICA
ON ACID-FREE PAPER
BY HADDON CRAFTSMEN, BLOOMSBURG, PENNSYLVANIA

For Pete, always.

## Chapter One

Each deliberate boot stomp descending the garage apartment steps made Terri Page flinch. The revved pickup motor, stones peppering the side of the building, dashed all hope that Daryl Durand would have the decency not to spin out. Stunned, her mood veered from hurt to anger. Fury choked her. When the phone jangled, she nearly came out of her skin.

"McDonnell Stables," she managed, lips trembling.

"Come to my office," octogenarian Alfred McDonnell ordered, his voice ricocheting off her ear drum. "Hurry along. I have a surprise for you!"

"S-surprise?" she sputtered.

Alfred hung up.

Silently she vowed to glue in his hearing aid.

Surprise? The grapevine gossip line at the stables had

already provided one. A tough one. The revelation of Daryl Durand's wife. Reverberations of the confrontation continued to make her tremble and rattle her senses. *How dare he try to use me. Who does he think he is?*

She drew in a sharp breath. Tears gathered. *And I was going to make . . . make a commitment to that lying, traitorous, deceiving jerk. What does he care about the truth? What does that say about me? Am I that . . . that gullible?*

Garnering deep embedded grit, grit that had been tested before, she took a stand. Never again would she tolerate anyone who wasn't upfront and honest. That helps, she thought. State it. Stand by it. Still the close call numbed her. She couldn't move. Alfred wanted her in his office, and she couldn't bring herself to budge. The moment was too raw.

In a motel near McDonnell Equestrian Complex, Robert Bromwell DVM rinsed the last trace of Midnight Magic hair dye down the drain. The nasty stuff had irritated his scalp. He hoped the roots were covered. Closing in on the mirror, nose almost touching the glass, he positioned a black-brown eyebrow pencil. A few awkward strokes and his sandy brows disappeared.

From the glossy countertop, he picked up a pair of fake glasses with black plastic rims. Clark Kent crossed his mind as he adjusted the frames on his face. If this is what Alfred wants then so be it, he told himself. How was he to know when he jokingly mentioned a disguise he'd take him up on it? He couldn't refuse. Not when he owed so much to his mentor.

Sifting through the contents of a burgundy briefcase, RDB initialed in gold in the corner, he found the computer printout of Clay Moore Equine Transportation, Satisfaction Guaranteed, boldly printed across the top. Cell phone in hand, he mouthed a silent request to the ceiling and beyond that the hearing aid was in place. Alfred answered in a normal voice.

"This is Robert. I'm leaving for your office now."

"Have you, er, got it on?"

Robert chuckled. "You bet. Clay Moore is my pseudonym. Remember the Lone Ranger played by Clayton Moore. Think of me as the masked do-gooder."

"Thanks for cooperating," Alfred said. "I've gone to a lot of trouble keeping my adversary in the dark."

"I know," Robert agreed. "There's another factor too. If the horse people involved knew who I was, I'd be swamped. This showdown is going to attract the sports media too."

"That worries me. You'll need a free rein. No distractions."

He glanced at the computer printout. "I've got official-looking credentials."

"Good. You'll be hauling the horse from Fresno to Fiddle, Texas. In my opinion it'll take five days."

"What's the rider like?"

"Her name is Terri Page. She's a real sweetheart.

Came up the ranks the hard way. Nobody knows her either."

"Does *she* know who I am?" he asked, hope in his voice.

"No!" Alfred barked. "The fewer people who know your identity, the happier I'll be. I want you to swear you won't reveal it."

"Swear to it?" Robert repeated, mildly shocked.

"That's right, Robert. This showdown has been under wraps for a long time. I don't want to risk a foul up. Every aspect of it has to be a complete surprise to Cora."

Humoring his old friend, he declared, "I swear."

"You mean it?" Alfred questioned.

"You bet. You know Texans. Our word is gospel."

"Is that it then?" Alfred asked.

"Not exactly. I plan to do research on the side."

"Research on what?" Alfred demanded, alarm in his voice.

Robert responded with confidence. "There's been a wave of studies lately on science-designed diets for athletes, high energy, peak performance, that sort of thing. I want to know if diets can affect the rider during competition."

"You do one thing to upset my rider, and I'll have your hide," Alfred warned.

"I won't. Trust me. She'll never know."

Alfred ignored his remarks. "I'll have your hide drawn and quartered. You can take *that* to the bank."

Treading on touchy ground, Robert dropped the subject and said his good-byes. Robert Bromwell DVM, alias Clay Moore, picked up his duffel bag, briefcase, and eyebrow pencil and turned off Fox News. Whistling a little tune, he shut the motel door behind him.

Terri forced herself into action. On the way to the bathroom she grabbed a purple sweatshirt from the back of a lumpy brown recliner. Popping her head through the neck, she struggled with the sleeves. To steady herself she clutched the edge of the porcelain basin and focused on the rusty drainage circle. *Calm down, be tough,* she told herself. *Alfred's up to something and I need to be ready.*

Twisting shoulder-length tresses into a bun, she felt her boiling point rising. Daryl said my hair was the color of a desert sunset, all gold and red. What does that liar know? Desert sunsets are orange, purple, and pink. Jabbing a bobby pin in place, she shook her head to make sure the bun stayed in place. An unexpected burst of gut-wrenching tears followed.

She cupped her hands under the spigot and let the cold water run through her fingers until the skin shriveled. At the last moment she splashed the salty tears from her face. A quick glance in the mirror attached to the rickety medicine cabinet above the sink revealed a splotchy complexion. Hastily she applied a film of tawny foundation. A final check produced a frown. *This purple shirt brings out the worst. I look like a grape.*

Racing down the garage apartment steps, she kept her chin tucked and her thoughts on Alfred, the most respected and, clearly, the most eccentric horseman in the business. His reputation for executing the surprise element on the competition was legendary. Curiosity kicking in, she wondered if Green Luck, the gray Irish thoroughbred, was involved.

The infamous Fresno fog closing in on the complex blurred the edges of the enclosed arena ahead. In the background, a horse whinnied. A whip snapped. Banter echoed. The dark-haired stranger emerging from a pickup parked in front of the arena briefly caught her attention. In passing she watched him showing patience with the gimpy-legged barn cat in his path. The scene, barely brushing across her vision, stirred a chord and brought a smile.

At the glass-paneled door, hand on the chrome bar, she paused. Beyond her own hazy reflection she could see Alfred McDonnell hunkered behind the mammoth oak desk. Taking a deep breath, she walked forward.

"Good evening!" Alfred shouted.

Leaning over the desk, Terri smiled at her employer. In the same swift motion she dipped her hand in his shirt pocket. "Here you go," she said, handing him the hearing aid.

Tapping the flesh-colored object in place, McDonnell announced several decibels lower, "It's showdown time."

The door swished open and closed. "Showdown?"

she questioned, slightly perplexed and a little annoyed at the intrusion behind her.

"Cora and I are going to duke it out."

The whole equestrian world knew Cora Stuart and Alfred McDonnell were archrivals, but duke it out? Astounded, her eyes popped. Following Alfred's gaze, she turned to face the newcomer. He was closer to her than she'd expected.

Respecting Alfred's penchant for secrecy and the fact he'd just dropped a bomb, she felt it her duty to take care of the situation. Taking charge, she asked, "Can I help you?"

The stranger towered over her. Dressed in faded jeans and a worn denim Western shirt, he merely smiled down at her. The black wavy locks lapping his collar caught her eye, but it was the teasing grin that bore watching. Behind the funky, heavy-rimmed glasses a pair of amusing gray eyes assessed her. She could feel the scrutiny and, in return, lifted her chin.

"Can I help you?" she repeated, pursing her lips.

"Perhaps Alfred can introduce us." Raising one dark brow at her, he turned his attention to the octogenarian behind the desk.

Indignant, Terri looked to Alfred too.

"Let me see now," Alfred stalled. Craning her neck, she tried to read off the computer paper the interloper had slipped under his nose. "Yes, yes," Alfred continued. "Clay Moore. This is Terri Page, the rider you will be assisting."

Terri turned back to Clay. His eyebrow shot up further. "Assistant?" she asked, her voice rising in bewilderment.

"You bet," he answered calmly.

Annoyed this perfect stranger knew more than she did, Terri frowned. "What is going on? Assistant for what?"

Alfred leaned back and clasped his gnarled hands over his belt buckle. "Showdown time. It's going to be a real wing-dingy. Pull up a chair."

Terri glanced in the direction of the round conference table and the chrome and black leather chairs. Before she could move Clay had crossed the room and had the chairs in hand. She waited for him to place them side by side in front of the oak desk.

As soon as they were seated Alfred began slowly, savoring each word. "Cora and I are going to settle it once and for all. We've been competing for over forty years. Before it's too late we're going head to head. One class will decide it all. This will take place in Fiddle, Texas, at Jake Bob Johnson's arena. That's why, uh, uh—"

Robert stepped up to the plate. "Clay Moore, your horse hauler and handler, is on board."

Alfred coughed. "Cora and I have set up our own rules. One class, one rider, one horse, and one assistant. The assistant can be anybody except a trainer. In other words"—he blinked his watery round hazel eyes at both of them—"no last minute surprises."

The information sank like a ton of bricks. A million questions began to crisscross her brain. "Green Luck is the horse, right?"

Alfred nodded. "The class will be the puissance wall."

Terri gulped. A quick flash of a solid structure of hollow blocks popped up in her head. Blocks would be added until they failed to clear it. "And Clay is to be my assistant?" she asked in disbelief.

"The one and only," Alfred confirmed.

"Why?" she exclaimed in a spontaneous outburst. "Why can't we use someone from the staff familiar with Greenie?"

"The horse has to be hauled to Texas. Clay is in the horse transportation business. There's no need for you to worry. He'll do fine as your assistant."

Terri faced Clay. His gray eyes behind the funky frames held her in such a way that she flushed. Head tucked, she checked the toes of her paddock boots. Unexpectedly she became aware of the horrible purple shirt and her tangerine complexion.

"That's me all right."

His voice, deep and melodious, made her shiver.

"Horse hauler and attendant for the Super Bowl of all showdowns," he finished with a smile.

Alfred chuckled. His attention focused on Terri. "I want you to work Green Luck in the morning. You'll be leaving at noon tomorrow."

She blanched. "So soon?"

"Cora and I had to synchronize the availability of Jake Bob's arena with the course designer's schedule."

Terri wasn't quite finished. "I suppose Cora will show Bewick Swan with Roy Scott in the irons?"

"That's her plans," Alfred replied, hardly able to contain himself. "Cora's never seen Green Luck."

"Or me either," Terri groaned.

"Me either," Clay chimed in.

"Keep 'em guessing," Alfred snorted, right proud of himself. "After the workout, we'll have a short meeting to go over the final details."

Rooted to the chair Terri watched Alfred open the desk side drawer and withdraw the latest edition of the horse travel guide and two maps. Handing them to Clay, he said, "It'll take five days in my opinion. Horse motels are available in Mojave, Flagstaff, Albuquerque, Amarillo, and Dallas. I'll leave it up to you two to make reservations. From Dallas to Fiddle takes less than two hours. Route 40 seems to be . . ."

Barely conscious of the discussion going on between Clay and Alfred, Terri did her best to rationalize the situation. She felt she'd come too far and respected Alfred too much to challenge his decisions, but he was have trouble remembering this man's name. It raised the hairs on her arms. Like a gathering storm, a craving for comfort food came over her. A candy bar, chocolate with nuts, something she could bite down on.

When Clay's chair scraped and Alfred's feet shuffled, Terri stood. Clay held open the glass-paneled door for her. "I need to talk to you," she said, her voice stern. "We have a few things to go over."

"At your service," he drawled. "Your place or mine?"

"Mine," she stated abruptly. "We can make the reservations."

Clay nodded toward his pickup.

She pointed skyward to the garage apartment. Briskly, she started off. "Ever assisted a rider before?"

"Not exactly." His tone was apologetic.

Terri's stomach knotted. "It's not easy," she said, thinking this is not the time for a novice.

As if reading her mind, he moved closer to her. "I'm a fast learner. Trust me."

His hair gel caught her off guard. It smelled like ammonia mixed with horse liniment.

At the foot of the stairs, she stopped. Resting a foot on the first step, she said, "Come on. My apartment is upstairs."

Right behind her, he breathed, "Lead the way."

She took the next step faster.

Inside, he occupied most of the free standing space in the one-room apartment. Terri followed his line of vision from the clothes draped on the lumpy brown recliner to the stacked dishes on the counter and finally to the bed hogging the middle of the room. As usual her most-prized possessions, her riding clothes encased in clear plastic garment bags, hung neatly on the back of the door.

"If you're looking for a chair, you're standing in

it," she said brightly, tossing him a pillow from the bed. "Use it for a backrest."

One-handed he caught the missile. Stretching his long legs out in front of him, he adjusted the pillow against the bedstead. "Hmmmm . . . nice," he said, his voice jovial, almost musical.

"This apartment is part of my contract with Alfred. I mean he likes me right under his thumb when it comes to Green Luck. Now I see why. Good grief. He and Cora having it out. I get the shakes thinking about it. What if we mess up?"

"We won't," he assured her, his pitch soft and soothing.

Terri felt the vibrations of his voice coursing through her and, self-conscious of the sensation she had no control over, turned her back on him. At the counter she began opening a loaf of bread.

"Want a peanut butter and jelly sandwich?" she asked.

"No thanks. Is this your supper?"

"You could call it that."

Joining Clay on the floor, Terri munched away on the sandwich. Clay retrieved a pillow from the bed and adjusted it to her back. Mouth full, she nodded thanks.

"Got any suggestions?" he asked.

Terri shrugged and swallowed slowly. "Somehow between here and Fiddle we've got to come together as a team. You know, me, Green Luck, and you. Can you believe Alfred?"

"He's gone to a lot of trouble getting this showdown together without revealing his hand to Cora."

"That's his style. Never revealing his hand." Her voice took on the attitude of a drill sergeant. "And you better not let me down. Your job will be a combination of groom, gofer, keeping up with the schedule, and dealing with the unexpected. There's always the unexpected at a horse show. Sounds easy, but it isn't."

"I can handle it. Trust me."

*Trust him? Alfred can't even remember his name.* "Why haven't I seen you around?" she asked, unable to hide the skepticism in her question.

"My horse transportation business is fairly new." He began rattling the maps Alfred had given him. Spreading them across his knees he became totally absorbed in the state of California. "Alfred's right. Five stops."

"Now, wait a minute. You're a novice horse hauler and Alfred hired you?"

"I have a few other talents," Clay offered thumbing through the guide book. "Who has copies of Green Luck's health certificate? Is it up to date?"

Not letting him off the hook, Terri persisted. "Exactly what other talents?"

He peered at her over the glasses teetering on the end of his nose. "I'm a fair hand at handling horses. Plus like you and Green Luck, I'm an unknown. I believe Alfred's plan is to psych out Cora."

"That figures, but how much do you know about assisting a horse and rider during competition? I can see it now. You'll be off checking the scenery, and I'll need you to hand me a crop or tighten a girth. We *have* to think like a team."

"Don't worry. We've got time between here and Fiddle to get it together." His eyes, clear and observant, held her briefly. He added, "If you don't mind, I'll start on the horse motel reservations."

Terri nodded, and, brushing crumbs from her jeans, announced, "Since we're leaving tomorrow I need to do laundry. I won't have time in the morning. There's a washer-dryer downstairs." Still brushing crumbs, she tried to sound nonchalant. "Er, where did you meet Alfred?"

Punching numbers, Clay hushed her with his free hand.

Terri gathered clothes from the recliner, clambered out the door and down the stairs through the dense, clogging fog. When she reached the garage door, Wayne Rudd, Alfred's trainer, came up behind her and opened it for her.

Just a breath taller than Terri's five foot five inch frame, they were eye to eye. His wiry, tanned physique and bristly gray crew cut made his age undefinable. To Terri, his ability to train horses was insurmountable.

"The cat's out the bag," he stated. "Alfred told me."

"What do you think? I mean, we're leaving tomorrow!"

"Unless the unforeseen happens, The Luck won't

spook at the wall. The horse trusts you. What worries me is if Alfred retires what's going to happen to us?"

"Jeez, Rudd, I didn't think of that."

"Rumors are flying fast and furious at the stables."

"All I know is I'll do my best for Alfred. He rescued me from Bennington Stables. I owe him everything."

Rudd nodded. "I'd have passed away in obscurity on the East Coast if it weren't for Alfred."

Their eyes locked and the conversation halted. At last Terri sighed deeply. "What do you know about Clay Moore?"

"Not one thing," he replied, agitated. "Alfred's stonewalling on that one."

Over the whir of the washer she hung on to every last minute instruction he had to offer. When he paused for breath, she fired a dozen what-if questions at him. At last they both agreed Green Luck could, would, and must win . . . for all of them.

As Rudd was leaving he turned, faced Terri, and hesitated. "Uh, you okay? The ruckus and all."

Terri huffed. "I suppose the whole equestrian complex heard Daryl's departure."

"Well . . ."

"That dishonest jerk! He tried to use me." Voice tight, she repeated, "He tried his level best to use me."

"Take it easy," he said and paused. "Don't worry about details. I'll pack Green Luck's show trunk."

"Thanks. Thanks for everything. I wish you were going."

Worry-ridden, she'd come back later and switch to the dryer. Meanwhile, a strange man was in her apartment.

Slowly, she eased open the door. Clay was busy jotting notes in a little pad. Light from the cracked bathroom door sliced across the room. She could see the front of the medicine cabinet hanging by one hinge. The tall stranger in his well-fitted Western jeans, his expert haircut, looked devilishly handsome and totally out of place.

"Uh . . . hum." Terri shuffled her boots. "What are you doing? Making a list and checking it twice?"

Amusement flickered in the eyes that met hers. "Actually I'm devising an itinerary."

Terri wrinkled her brow. "Speaking of intineraries, did you have any trouble with the horse motel reservations?"

"All done and accounted for," he said tucking the notepad in his shirt pocket. "Each and every stable contacted was happy to rent a stall overnight to a McDonnell horse. I've written the confirmations on the inside of the travel guide. We'll find motels for ourselves along the way."

Terri followed his hands, long-fingered and strong, as they opened the guide. Fascinated by the movement and the lack of wasted motion, she did a double-take when he asked if she was feeling stressed. "Stress was not an option," flew out of her mouth before the thought could freeze in her brain.

Composure gained, she said, "I saw Wayne Rudd in the garage. He's taking care of details. The show trunk, I mean."

"Great. Is there anything I can do?"

"Tomorrow morning, five A.M. to be exact, I'm working Green Luck. Alfred wants him to stay on schedule as much as possible. Will you be there to assist?"

Capturing her eyes with his he said, "You bet."

Disconcerted, Terri began digging into her canvas tote bag. From the depths she brought forth two candy bars. "Here, have one."

"Candy bar? Peanut butter and jelly? That's not good."

"Who are you? The health police?"

"No," he admitted, "but you have to think of the caffeine and the sugar factor. It'll jitter your nerves. You want to win, don't you?"

Peeling back the wrapper, she said, "I'll compromise. One bite. That's all."

Clay shrugged. "Suit yourself."

Breaking off a huge hunk she passed the bar under his nose. "Mmmmmm, good. Sure you don't want some?"

Playfully he caught her hand and brought the clutched candy bar to the side of her face. "A perfect match."

Feeling responsible for his action, she freed her hand and rubbed the tingles where they'd touched. After all it was innocent joking around with Daryl that brought on more than she'd bargained for. Even so, she was curious.

"What match?"

"Your eyes are Snickers-brown." Leaning forward to examine them closer he began warbling, "Don't it make"—milking nuances and grinning—"my broooown eyes blue."

His far-too-dangerous voice sent up a red flag. "Yeah?" she fired back. "So's horse manure."

Clay's laughter floated up from his throat.

"Time to call it quits, Clay."

At the door Terri said good night twice before Clay began his descent down the stairs. Watching his tempting, attractive physique disappearing through the fog, she furrowed her brows when he stopped midway. Keeping his back toward her, he began gently crooning, "On the road again . . . I can't wait to get on the road again . . ."

The magical notes seemed to float up behind him sending a message she was positive she wanted to avoid.

## Chapter Two

The intermittent *dong*, *dong*, *dong* finally got to Terri. The pillow she had pulled over her head and over her ears didn't help. Finally she slapped the clock's off button and moaned. Slumped on the edge of the bed she pulled a long T-shirt over her head. On the way to the shower, she stubbed her toe on the recliner. McDonnell's blacksmith's creative name for an ornery horse slipped out.

As the steamy water streamed over her body, her subconscious nudged a nugget of information to the uppermost part of her mind. It became crystal clear why Alfred had sent her and Greenie to Ireland. They were getting ready for this showdown. The grueling courses at Haggarty Farms had prepared the horse and herself completely out of Cora Stuart's sight.

The business of Clay Moore continued to stump her. Alfred couldn't have known him long. He wasn't even sure of his name, but Alfred's in his eighties. He's entitled to forget. Somehow that didn't ring true. Not with a deal as big as this. Maybe, she shuddered, he's outdone himself.

Knowing this kind of thinking could drive her nuts, she congratulated herself for not allowing any serious brain chatter to sneak in about Daryl Durand. Double D. Double trouble. Instead she began belting out Willie's "On the road again. I can't wait to get on the road again."

Startled by a tap-tap she turned off the water. Rivulets of bubbly shampoo oozed down her body while she waited, frozen, for the unidentifiable noise to repeat itself. Silence. Shrugging, she vigorously turned the spigots full blast. Continuing on she hit the high notes with heartfelt verve.

Confident only keen-eyed eagles were privy to the tiny window above the sink, she paraded with a towel turban around her head to the lumpy brown recliner. Searching for underwear, she heard it again. *Tap. Tap. Tap.*

Frantically pulling a sweatshirt over her head, she called out, "Who is it?"

"Clay Moore."

"Just a minute." Praying he hadn't heard her rendition, she hop-skipped into a pair of sweatpants on her way to the door. Barely cracking it she poked out her nose. "Whatcha need?"

His smoky-gray eyes hiding behind the weird glasses teased mischievously. "May I come in?"

Withdrawing her nose, she opened the door and stepped aside. "What's on your mind?"

"Doing my job. Checking the schedule," he replied, easing his tall, athletic body inside.

Terri eyed the back of his faded jeans as he needled his way around a bag of trash, her backpack, and a stack of country and Western CDs. Toeing aside an English girth coiled at his feet, Clay folded his lanky body and sank to the floor. Reaching over his head for a pillow to prop against the bedstead, he smiled up at her.

"How did you sleep?" he asked as casually as if it were high noon at a Fourth of July picnic.

"Like a rock," she shot back. "I hope you understand I don't have time for a social call." The soggy towel around her head drooped on each side. In an attempt to rewind it, the towel took on a life of its own. "As for the schedule," she continued, her jaws a little tight, "we went over this last night. Work Greenie at five, meet with Alfred for final details. I don't even know who the scorekeeper is."

"Ross Shelton," Clay offered.

His knowledge annoyed her. "Oh?" she snapped. "How do you know that?"

She felt his eyes concentrating on her face, watchful of her expression.

"Alfred told me."

"Anything else?"

"Yes. How are you handling the pressure?"

Terri tapped her bare foot on the cold floor. "What are you playing? Mind games?"

Ignoring the question, Clay came up with one of his own. "What are you having for breakfast?"

Taken back, she narrowed her eyes. "Fudge."

Clay Moore rose to his full height and firmly placed his hand on her shoulder. "I'm taking you out for breakfast as soon as we're finished at the stables."

His voice was so commanding it threw her. She clamped her jaws shut to prevent the ugliest of all ugly comebacks from slipping out. Tension crackled the short space between them. Refusing to let the hand cupping her shoulder distract her, she gathered fortitude and glared him down.

"Alfred McDonnell did not hire you to be my nursemaid," she said, clipping her words.

"No, he did not," Clay agreed. "We have to use every weapon in the arsenal to win. I think you are aware a healthful diet would be beneficial." He gave her shoulder a gentle squeeze before removing his hand. In a kinder tone, he added, "I don't sign on with teams that don't give one hundred and ten percent."

Her jaw came close to hitting the floor. Dumbstruck she stared at him as he made his way around her and to the door. With his hand on the knob, he glanced over his shoulder. Wiggling both brows he began twanging, "On the road again . . . can't wait . . ."

Exasperated she threw the wet towel at him. The door slammed just in time for the towel to thud against the riding clothes hanging neatly on the back. Gaping at the missile sliding down the plastic garment bags, she could hear him laughing on the other side. The name she called him was not nice. Her only hope was he heard it.


The skylights above cast pinkish-gray diagonal patterns on the dark sandy arena floor. Crossing the area to the arch leading to the stalls, Terri inhaled deeply. This was her home. Every facet of the building and each and every four-legged occupant was precious to her. She loved it all. No matter how down she was, this was the place for a lifting of spirit, a sense of belonging.

On this particular morning, she marched on a mission. Apprehensive, she tried to shake the weight of the event pressing down on her. She began to devise a plan. If the practice session didn't go smoothly—and she was positive it wouldn't—she'd find the courage to tell Alfred to replace Clay. He wouldn't like it, but she thought he'd understand. She needed someone with more experience.

Through the arch and down the aisle, she glanced in each stall until she reached Green Luck's. Drawing in the familiar earthiness of warm horse flesh and the woodsy smell of the deep bedding of fresh shavings, she tapped on the bars of Greenie's stall. "Morning, handsome," she sang out. *Where is that jerk?*

"You don't look so bad yourself, buddy," he said emerging from the tackroom. He had Green Luck's saddle across his arm, the bridle slung over his shoulder.

"Buddy?" she threw back. A sidelong glance at his faked wounded expression quivered her lips. Turning from him, she concentrated on Green Luck's stall door latch.

"What do you think?" she asked businesslike. "Is this a great horse or what?"

Backing off, Clay carefully scrutinized the seventeen hands gray Irish thoroughbred. "He's got a short crested neck and a powerful behind," he observed thoughtfully. "Kind of gives the appearance of a giant pony."

Her eyes popped. "That's what Alfred says."

Approaching the horse, he motioned her aside while he slipped on the halter and clipped on the lead line. When he announced the horse was coming out she allowed him more space. His easiness in handling the horse was encouraging, but it was the gentle, quiet movement of his hands around the horse's head that truly impressed her.

In the aisleway he put the horse in the crossties. Turning in her direction, he asked, "Saddle time?"

"You got it."

Hugging her safety helmet, she leaned against the stall and prayed he'd make a mistake. Do something dumb. But it didn't take long to realize he had expertise or that Greenie was comfortable with him. In fact he had a rare talent not often seen in the horse world. *Be honest*, she told herself. *Scratch replacement. I'm the one not comfortable with him.*

When he'd finished she followed him as he led Green Luck down the aisleway, under the arch, and into the arena. Dead center the trio came to a stop.

"Leg up?" he asked. Holding the reins he moved to the horse's side.

"Thanks," she mumbled. Taking the reins from him she slipped them over Greenie's head, placed her hand on the front of the saddle, and crooked her leg under her. His firm grip propelled her smoothly up on the horse. Mounted she frowned at the distraction of his hand on her leg. *How many leg ups have I had?* she scolded herself. *Why does his have to be any different?*

Out the corner of her eye, she caught Alfred crossing the arena to join Clay. Pitching herself into a mode of focused concentration, she took Green Luck on the rail. After a warm-up, she faced the practice jump, cleared it, and brought the horse to a halt beside Alfred. Relaxing the reins she leaned over the saddle. Her brown eyes darkened in intensity as she waited for Alfred's critique.

His first comment, "Don't let your enthusiasm

overrule your determination to win," surprised her, but what tugged at her heart was his request for a winner's smile at the end. A winner's smile flitted across her thoughts. It didn't sound like Alfred. The slight puzzlement passed as quickly as a blink of the eye.

Following the work out, Terri, Clay and Alfred hunkered around the conference table. At the last minute, joined by Rudd, they got down to business. About to embark on a venture with one Clay Moore, Terri brought up the question of who was in charge of the expedition. Alfred responded by not really defining his answer, but implied they both were.

Terri cut her eyes at Clay, making sure he understood they were on equal ground. He mouthed *buddies*, punctuating the word with an arched brow. What she mouthed back raised both brows.

The whole deal was taking on such a tone of finality Terri wanted desperately to ask what his plans were after the showdown. With the score settled between Alfred and Cora, would his stables go by the wayside? She swallowed back the thought of her horse family scattering.

Alfred went on and on about Greenie's strong points. Rudd brought up Bewick Swan's vast experience in the show ring and the fact no one could ever rule out Roy Scott, a master in the irons. Terri scooted down in the chair, heart pounding in her ears. Was she ready?

Alfred closed the meeting with the announcement

he'd arrive at Jake Bob's the day before the event. His final orders to Clay were to call each night with a report and to leave a travel itinerary on his desk. With that he stood and began handing out credit cards and envelopes of cash.

Terri dawdled at the door. Taking a deep breath, she reentered the room. "Will there be any spectators?"

"A few," Alfred replied. He was about to elaborate when the phone rang. She prayed the exchange would be brief.

"Cora, old gal, how are you this morning?" Settling down in his chair, he snort-cackled. "Care to make a wager?"

Slowly she backed out the room. Clay, waiting for her, blocked her exit. "Don't touch the fudge. I'm taking you out for real food."

"Excuse me?" Her lips pursed.

"I have a couple of things to do," he said as if nothing was possibly out of line. "I'll meet you at the apartment."

His audacity incensed her. Watching his backside retreating, she thought he had the nerve of a jerk. *Who does he think he is? I'm not going to put up with this.*

Clay found privacy in Alfred's office. Sitting on the edge of the desk, he faced the door. Cell phone plastered to his ear, he waited through six beeps.

"Bromwell Clinic, Doctor Eakin speaking."

"What's going on?"

"Robert! Man, how did you handle it by yourself?"

"That's why I hired you." Robert chuckled, thinking it was time he'd learned to delegate some of the workload at the clinic. Tony Eakin filled the bill. "Give it to me slow."

"Six horses are coming in for Coggins tests. I've been out to Murray's farm. His mule got hung up in a barb-wire fence, nine sutures. I'm checking the wound tomorrow for infection. Old Man Coleman calls daily about his stallion. He wants to talk to you and you only."

"Don't let him get to you. Every time the horse passes gas he thinks he needs surgery."

Tony sighed. "Your secretary—"

"Our secretary."

"Our secretary, Tracy, left early because of boyfriend problems. The lab tech is helping out with the phone."

"Hey, we're a team at the clinic. I'll be back by the end of the week."

"No sweat," Tony said. "Of course, we're not speculating over all this secrecy."

Robert laughed. "I'm not taking the bait. Sounds like you've got everything under control. I'll check in periodically. Don't call unless it's life or death."

As soon as he hung up, he folded his arms across his chest and smiled. The lifting of the burden of his practice was having a strange effect on him. No, it wasn't easy sharing his life's work with a wet-behind-the-ears vet, but it was the smartest thing he'd ever done.

What is this? A mid-life crisis? Living the life of a workaholic has its rewards. A clinic to be proud of and clients who depended on him. The down side, no time for a social life. I feel like a kid out of school. She's got to be in her twenties and here I am on the down side of thirty five. Terri is as bluntly honest as you can get and here I am posing as a masked do-gooder. Ingrained in his DNA is the idea that a Texan was only as good as his word and he'd given his word to Alfred. He eased off the desk and headed for the apartment.

It all started in the restaurant when he leaned across the booth and cupped his hand over hers. Holding her with his clear gray eyes he plainly stated, "The pancakes and syrup won't do."

The disturbing contact made her want to fight back with a smart remark. Instead, knowing sugar was her preferred go-to food, she asked in a grudging tone, "What do you suggest?"

"Oatmeal with a side dish of fresh fruit." His hand still covering hers began patting it.

It was the same as saying good girl. Yanking free from his touch, she growled, "Is coffee allowed?"

Clay chuckled. "Up to you. I might as well warn you, once we get rolling I don't make many pit stops."

Thrusting back her shoulders she lifted her chin.

"Maybe I should ride in the trailer with Green Luck. That way—" The waitress at her elbow prevented the conclusion of what she thought would put him in his place.

During the meal she did her best to extricate information regarding his transportation business. She thought it strange he didn't have one anecdote to tell. Every horse person she'd ever known had at least one favorite experience to share. He seemed more interested in what she ate.

During the ride back to the stables she remained quiet. Studying the sand in the crevices of the floor mat, she wondered if she was being paranoid because Clay was so secretive. At least, she conceded, he isn't lying. He just isn't sharing.

At the first glimpse of the truck the McDonnell Stables' staff bolted from the wide doors and lined up in front of the arena. Jumping up and down they waved hastily made cardboard signs marked with BE-WICK SWAN'S SWAN SONG and KEEP 'EM GUESSING. Waving in the breeze a computer-designed banner displayed the stables motto, JUST JUMP IT.

Terri bounded from the truck, arms spread. The laughter, banter, and comebacks bounced between them as she hugged each and every one. Missing Rudd in the mix she began backing off.

She found him in the tack room setting out a tray of doughnuts next to the giant coffee urn used for special occasions. One glance at the pastries and Terri cried, "After my own heart!"

Reaching for a cream-filled puffy concoction she leaned back against a saddle rack and smacked her lips. It went down so easily she picked up another. Rudd took this opportunity to give her last-minute instructions. Vastly interested in the information and trying hard to memorize every word, she absentmindedly popped a miniature chocolate éclair in her mouth.

The commotion in the aisleway picked up. Terri, the honoree, touched Rudd's arm. Looking in his eyes with a multitude of unspoken gratitude, she murmured, "Thanks for all your patient training. I'll try to do you proud."

Rudd nodded. "Good luck."

Grinning, styrofoam cup in hand, Terri mounted the hay bale in front of Greenie's stall. "Here! Here!" she exclaimed, individually tipping the cup in acknowledgement to each member of the staff crowded around. "To the world's greatest manure shovelers, mane braiders, grooms, fellow riders, and trainer. Green Luck will whup the Swan's as . . . astronomical behind! Anybody here know Bewick Swan's swan song?"

From the back of the aisle, Clay Moore materialized. Somewhere along the way he'd confiscated a black Resistol. The brim rode low on his forehead. Flashing a devilish grin at Terri, he cupped his hands over his mouth and began whistling "Taps." By using his palm as an echo factor he made each mournful note sound like a bugle gone bad.

Horses shuffled uneasily in the stalls. Downright laughter broke out. Terri's twitter was a nervous reaction. She knew that. No way could she let these people down. They were family.

On the last note Clay swept off the Resistol and took a bow. The staff huddled around him firing questions. Terri tried to catch his answers, but all she heard was ". . . Texas born and raised . . . leaving at noon." Eventually horse-related chores took precedence and the crowd drifted away. Slipping his arm around her waist he affirmed the inevitable close to her ear, "Time to head 'em up and move 'em out."

The tingle of excitement racing through her veins had to be caused by the impending event, she told herself. But to be safe she shifted her stance and studied her nails. "I'm all packed. Anytime you're ready."

"Soon as I hitch the trailer to my truck, I'll meet you at the garage," he said backing off. "It won't take long."

Terri paced the floor. At the last minute she remembered the vitamin pills. One of these days this medicine cabinet door is going to bite the dust, she thought as she raked the bottles into her shoulderbag.

Tires crunched gravel.

She heard him bounding steps two at a time.

He insisted on carrying down all of her luggage,

the plastic garment bags, boots, and helmet. She grabbed the CD case and clutched it to her breasts. Dancing first on one foot and then the other, she scrutinized his placement of her backpack on the extended cab's bench. Behind the driver's seat tucked in the opposite corner contained his duffel bag.

Hitched to his emerald-green Dodge, Alfred's jet-black trailer with McDonnell Stables etched in gold on the side had separate dressing and tack compartments across the front. At the back were two side-by-side stalls. Methodically, Clay hung her riding clothes on the hooks in the dressing compartment and arranged her boots in the corner while Terri observed over his shoulder.

Unable to stand still, she peeked inside the tack compartment. All of the tack, both working and show, hung neatly on the rack. One glimpse inside the show trunk told her Rudd had indeed packed it. The placement of the equipment and medical supplies had his signature.

Rocking back and forth on her heels, she waited for Clay to finish. Finally he shut the dressing room door and jiggled the handle. Next he rechecked the tack compartment.

"Driver," she asked smartly, "may I put my CDs under the passenger's side seat?"

"Of course, madam horse-rider extraordinaire. Are we having a sugar reaction?"

"It's mademoiselle," she corrected.

Looking her in the eye, he French twisted *pardon*. "And what about the sugar?"

Something in his eyes demanded an answer. "I only had three doughnuts." Hating to be trapped, she knew the tops of her ears were red. "And so what if I did?"

"A healthful diet is important," he responded his tone stern.

She couldn't argue with that.

On the short ride to the rear of the stables she tried stuffing the CD case under the seat. Something blocked it. Reaching under the seat she pulled up a burgundy leather briefcase. The initials RDB intrigued her.

"Whose is this?" she asked showing him the case.

"It belongs to my partner," he replied, clipping his words. "Toss it in the back."

"Partner of what? Your company?"

"Of course," he answered, definitely annoyed.

Focusing his attention on backing the trailer to the rear entrance of the arena stall section he eased to a stop. Terri watched and again was taken by his movements and the total lack of wasted motion. Soon she would be traveling halfway across the United States with this man. More annoyed than worried, she knew Alfred approved of his character or he wouldn't have hired him. She didn't want to think about his lapse of memory over his name.

Ambling through the back entrance to the stall section she found Rudd with Green Luck in the crossties clucking over him like a mother hen.

"I'll be glad when this is over," he said with a sigh. "I can't sleep thinking about it." Systematically he picked up each hoof and ran his thumb over every nail head. "My ulcer hasn't acted up in five years and now it's starting to. I'm driving Maggie bonkers. I guess you know how much is riding on this."

Feeling his anxiety transferring to herself she tried to make light of it. "Aw, come on. Green Luck will fly over the wall with inches . . . no . . . make that miles. Watch out moon." Working at keeping enthusiasm in her voice she added, "Think there'll be trophy in this?"

Rudd let go of the hoof, straightened up, and scratched the back of his neck. "My head, probably."

"Gimme a break!" She tried to laugh, but a gulp of air produced a hiccup. Not trusting her voice she gave him a thumbs up and headed back outside where Clay was preparing to load bales of lush alfalfa.

"Does Green Luck travel on the left side?" he asked.
Terri nodded.

Leaning against the building she watched him heft the bales. When he spread eagled his arms to grip the edge of the right side stall she came forward. "Need some help?"

"I got it," he called over his shoulder, shoving the bales tightly together with his boot heel. Stepping back he bumped into Terri. "Sorry," he apologized extending a hand to steady her. "Are you okay?"

Terri told him yes, but she wasn't sure. The unexpected contact was unnerving. Grateful for the familiar clip-clop of a horse, she pivoted in the direction of Rudd leading Green Luck to the trailer. While he gave Clay last minute instructions, she made a final pit stop. When she returned Clay was beside the truck cradling the old cat in his arms. His thumb pressed the bone in the gimpy hind leg.

She ruffled the cat's fur. "Rudd named him Festus." Looking up at Clay, she asked, "Are we ready?"

Clay hesitated. Gently releasing Festus to the ground, he cocked his head and observed the cat meander off. "How long has his leg been like that?"

Terri shrugged. "Ever since he showed up."

"It can be fixed, you know."

"It'd be nice," she said starting for the door. "Ready?"

"Have we got everything?"

"I think so."

Snapping his heels together, he thrust an imaginary torch to the sky. "Let the games begin!"

His booming voice rippled up her spine.

## Chapter Three

Barely out of sight of the McDonnell Equestrian Complex, Terri gathered Green Luck's health records and registration papers from the dashboard. She glanced over her shoulder.

"Where is it?"

"Where's what?"

She leaned over the seat to look on the floor. "The briefcase. It was on the back bench."

"I gave it to Rudd to give to Alfred."

Terri searched her brain for a clue. "When?"

"While you were taking a pit stop prior to blast off."

Slipping the papers in the door panel pocket she mumbled that the briefcase would've been a perfect place to keep Greenie's papers. Next she fiddled with the strap of her canvas shoulderbag. Finally she pitched it over the seat and on to the bench behind her. The contents of the bag shook, rattled, and rolled.

Terri squirmed. "Vitamin pills. See? I do care about my health. It's not as easy as you think."

"How so?" The interest in his voice was hard to deny.

"If I'm in the middle of a training session with Rudd I can't very well say 'oops, time for a nutrition break.' So I take vitamins." Her tone became deadly. "The bottom line is we have to think like a team."

"Team Wing-Dingy," he sang.

"I don't like it," Terri stated flatly.

He feigned surprise. "What don't you like?"

"The name. Granted wing-dingy is Alfred's favorite expression, but it's not . . . not appropriate. We need something more serious, more positive."

"Team," he boomed ominously, "Life or Death."

Reminded of his Bewick Swan's swan song, she giggled. "Please, we don't need to go that far."

"I like Wing-Dingy," he expounded thoughtfully. "It puts the showdown in perspective." He tapped her knee. "Lighten up."

Terri glared at his fingertips.

Ignoring the glare Clay returned his hand to the steering wheel. "What about Team Win? Short for wing-dingy."

She bobbed her chin. "Better."

Leaving Terri to her own thoughts, he wondered if the disguise wasn't such a bad idea after all. The last thing she needed was more distractions. He only hoped he could pull it off without making an idiot of himself, Terri, or Alfred. If someone had told him his presence at the Nationals would've caused so much commotion he wouldn't have believed it. He was there to scope Bewick Swan for Alfred not to be swamped by the equestrian crowd hammering him for his opinion on a horse ailment or to sign copies of his latest book, *Ten Tips To Conquer Colic*. He'd promised Alfred he'd keep an eye on Green Luck. The horse definitely had a sensitive stomach. He hoped his expertise in that field didn't let him down.

Terri appeared too tense to suit him. He could certainly relate to the pressure. Besides the weight of the showdown on her shoulders she's worried they wouldn't be a team. He dwelled on the team aspect until the horse was completely out the picture. Smiling he tooled on down the road.

Terri hunched against the door and folded her arms around her. She wanted to pinch herself. Out of all choices Alfred had picked her to settle the score with Cora. It quivered her nerves.

Drifting back to the first time she'd met Alfred, she smiled. He must've thought I had some nerve to ask him, the Alfred McDonnell, to wait, but the staff at Bennington Stables had gone to a show and had left her in charge. In the middle of feeding, she had to finish before she could bring out the mare he wanted to see.

Recalling times at Bennington Stables always made her wonder whatever happened to her bike. The one Bette, her grandmother, had given her on her eleventh birthday. The one she'd pedaled after school down the sandy lane, past Bette's beauty shop sign, through the walnut grove to the backside of Bennington Stables.

She could hear the trainer's voice as clearly as if he was in the cab with her. "Here, girl"—he'd always called her girl—"if you clean the tack, I'll give you a free riding lesson." "Girl, muck out the stall before the owner gets here. It'll be worth another lesson. You need work on picking up leads."

She fast-forwarded to when Alfred rescued her and put her on his top-of-the-line equines. Now here she was heading toward victory or defeat with one Clay Moore, an assistant she didn't know a thing about.

Getting back on track, she asked, "Did you say you'd been to Jake Bob's arena?"

"You bet." Glancing her way, he shoved the black frames up on his nose. "Actually the arena is a lot like Alfred's. The Luck should feel right at home."

In an attempt to ferret out more information, she went one step further. "When were you there?"

"About a month ago." Before she could ask why, he added, "I had to pick up a horse."

His tone did not encourage a discussion. Terri

chewed on it. From his looks he's probably thirty-something. So what did he do before he got in the horse transportation business? Where did he get his horse background? Why is he so tight-lipped? She started with, "You're from Texas, right?"

"Yep." That's as far as he went. Taking up the slack he tweaked a smile at her and modulated a perfect John Wayne "pilgrim."

Ignoring the diversion, Terri cut straight to the bone. "Where in Texas?"

"Outside of Dallas." He clamped his lips shut.

How vague can you get? "Is that where you learned to handle horses? Outside of Dallas?"

"You could say that. And Terri Page came up the ranks the hard way. Alfred told me all about you."

"It's not like Alfred to confide in someone whose name he can't remember." She figured that'd stump him.

"Alfred's eighty-five," he reminded her. "Lapses happen."

The sincerity of his voice rang true, especially when she was inclined to agree with him. She'd noticed Alfred dozing off, but never when it came to horses. Curiosity pecking away she probed lightly. "What else did he tell you?"

"That you're a real sweetheart."

Fluffing aside the remark, she shifted in the seat.

Out of the blue, he proclaimed, "Team Roy Roger? Or Roger Roy versus Team Win. Got any strategy?"

"Team who? What are you talking about?"

In control of the conversation, he explained, "Roger Hill is the farrier for Cor—"

"I've heard of Roger Hill. He's a top-notch blacksmith. Is he Roy Scott's assistant?"

Checking the mirror at a low-slung sports car coming up on him, he hesitated. Terri answered for him. "Yep." She turned her attention to the window. As if on cue they responded in unison. "Alfred told me." Terri twisted around to catch Clay's reaction.

He grinned at her. "See? Already we're thinking like a team. We keep this up, and we'll whup the Swan's astronomical behind off the map."

"I can't argue with that." Her voice was strong, but she couldn't leave it alone. Roy Scott and the Swan were great with or without Roger Hill, a knowledgeable blacksmith. One who could expertly handle any horse under any circumstances. And here she was with a green assistant. At a critical moment he could forget a piece of equipment. Screw her up big time.

To ease her mind, she asked, "What did you do before you and your partner started this horse transportation business?"

"I worked around. Different barns. That sort of thing."

Terri wanted details. "I know you never trained horses because that's in the rules."

"Ranch work is the best description. I've worked at

quite a few. Actually"—he continued getting into the description—"I've met a lot of horse people, traveled all over Texas picking up all sorts of knowledge along the way."

Drifter stabbed her gut. He's a drifter just like Daryl. Barns attract them. How did Alfred ever get tangled up with him? Then there's Alfred's hang-up. If he's kept Cora in the dark about Green Luck and me, surely he wouldn't have picked an assistant Cora knew. Keep 'em guessing. Somehow it fits. Somehow it's got to.

"Care to share a candy bar?" she asked, dragging her shoulderbag from the back bench.

"Sure."

Terri hid her surprise. Breaking the chocolate covered peanut bar in half she held up the pieces side by side and kept the shortest one.

"You know, Terri," he started.

Here it comes, she thought. Sugar, poor diet, something.

"Too much sugar can do a number on you."

"You're infuriating," she said, her voice quiet, deadly. "And for your information, I've eaten candy bars all my life and yet to fall off a horse because of it."

"I've heard digestion stops during competitive exercise, which means the energy the sugar provides does not go to the muscles or the brain."

Gleefully, she replied, "Which proves my point. The sugar just sits there not hurting anybody."

"Not so. I've also heard muscles need water during exercise and sugar draws body water into the stomach and away from muscles."

"Is that a fact?" she retorted, sniffing the air. "I've always heard sugar gives you a burst of energy."

Wadding up the candy wrapper, she searched for a place to dispose of it. Spying the ashtray, she pulled it open. Inside a black shiny eyebrow pencil, gold tipped on the end, laid crossways. She could feel the heat of Clay's gaze on her hand.

"Belong to your wife?" she asked, pointing to the pencil.

"Not married," Clay replied stiffly. "Just drop the wrapper on top."

"Ever?"

"Nope."

Terri thought, *I've heard that before.*

"I realize you have a lot on your mind, Terri."

She shot him a funny look. "Is this a pep talk?"

Exasperated he said, "Why don't you take a power nap?"

Twisting and turning she hauled her backpack over the seat and socked an indentation in the center for a pillow. Scrunching around to get comfortable, she could feel Clay's eyes on her. A whole minute passed and she didn't move.

"Okay?" he murmured, tucking a wayward golden-red strand behind her ear.

The gentle motion triggered a warm, soothing reaction that spread across her face. Rising up she mashed the backpack again and settled back down.

Scrambling upright, she rubbed her eyes. "Where are we?"

"Welcome to the Mojave Desert," Clay announced like a tourist guide. "*Mojave* means "three mountains" which is in reference to the needlelike formations of western Arizona."

*Does this man ever let up? I think he's a frustrated actor.* "We're still in California," she reminded him. Finger-combing her hair, she glanced around. "How close are we to the horse motel?"

"Very close," he replied, exiting off Route 40.

Beyond the waves of sand a range of unremarkable brown mountains broke the lavender-and-gold-streaked sky. A chicken-wire fence supported by weather-bleached posts cast checkered shadows across the secondary road. Horse rigs, one motor home, and a portable john materialized on the right. On the left were more chicken-wire fence and a scattering of sheds and stables.

Clay pulled in beside the rigs. "What do you think?"

"If the stalls aren't secure and the people aren't decent, we're not leaving Green Luck."

"This place is recommended in the horse travel guide. Says it rents stalls to travelers, excellent care. They've even provided the phone number of a local vet and farrier."

Terri gave him a questioning look. "Doesn't matter what they say. It'd better be safe."

As soon as boots hit the ground Green Luck stomped, rocking the trailer. Like a well-greased machine they made quick work of unloading the magnificent gray gelding. Handing her the lead line, Clay announced he was going to check the stables. With the horse papers hiked up under his arm, he started across the road. She couldn't help studying his backside and jaunty step.

When he returned with a wheelbarrow, he assured her the accommodations were adequate, decent, and up to par. He noted the working ring was small, but doable.

Curiously she observed his hands as they loaded Greenie's supplies into the wheelbarrow. Oddly struck by the lack of calluses and disjointed knuckles, she compared them to Rudd's. They weren't the hands of a horseman. Fingers that had never been caught and jerked by a pair of reins. In fact his strong, slender fingers were straighter than hers.

The shed row of eight stalls were tidily appointed with a feed bin, hay rack, water bucket, and fresh bedding. The top half of the stall doors were left open for air circulation. The proprietor sported a Santa Claus beard, wore jeans and a white T-shirt under an unbuttoned red flannel shirt. He introduced himself as Buckshot, the proprietor.

Inside the stall Clay had almost finished the task of

settling Greenie, when he called out, "Anybody next door?"

Terri moved over and peeked in. "A Shetland"—pausing long enough to check—"mare." The little pony pinned back its ears. "She looks old as dirt and as ornery as they come."

Buckshot laughed. "Ever seen a Shetland that wasn't? Tell ya one thing though, they'll be buddies before the night is over."

Buckshot recommended a motel for them in Gingham, a small town closeby. Clay and Terri gave him their cell phone numbers. They took turns asking him to call if there was a problem. He promised he'd keep an eye on the horse. In fact, he added, he'd be up most of the night waiting on stunt actors coming in from Hollywood to film a promotional video.

Before starting back toward the truck, she took one last look at Green Luck. Used to plenty of neighbors at the complex, he was already hugging the wall separating himself from the pony.

Trailer unhitched, doors to the compartments secured, they headed for Gingham. Terri pointed out the blinking motel sign on the barren landscape. Security lights splashed an eerie blue cast over the narrow structure. Clay pulled up by the office.

"I'll register," he said, cutting the key. "It looks like they have plenty of vacancies."

Terri nodded. The only vehicle in the lot was a rusted-out white pickup with a COWGIRLS RULE bumper sticker. Catty-corner to the motel loomed a restaurant that appeared to have seen better days. In the hazy plate glass window a neon outline of a boot, part of the spur burned out, sputtered. In front two old out-of-commission gas pumps stood like sentinels. If there was anymore to Gingham, she couldn't see it. Both the motel and the restaurant appeared to be abandoned in the expanse of the desert.

Clutching keys, Clay made quick work of sliding behind the wheel. "We're on the end," he said with foreboding in his voice. "Rooms 14 and 15."

Easing the nose of the truck in front of Room 15 he handed Terri a key dangling from a scarred circle of wood branded with the number 15. Inside she wrinkled her nose at the lingering smell of cigarette smoke mixed with pine oil disinfectant. Clay deposited her luggage on a rickety stand, her backpack on the floor. He began backing out the door.

"Give me fifteen minutes," he said, hand on the knob. "I need to check in with Alfred, Buckshot the proprietor, and make a few transportation business calls."

Alone she punched in Rudd's number and counted ten rings. Next she tried the main office, to no avail. Disappointed there'd be no information forthcoming concerning Clay Moore, she perched dejectedly on the edge of the bed. Any stable news would've been welcomed. *Whoever heard of being homesick for a stable? What is wrong with me?* At the first tap, she crossed the room and opened the door. Unexpectedly Clay's infectious grin lifted her spirits.

A devilish look came into his eyes. "Shall we try the busted boot cuisine?"

"Why not?" Terri felt her cheeks warm.

They headed diagonally across the parking lot toward the restaurant entrance. Boots crunched, thighs accidentally brushed. The moon winked at them and the stars twinkled close enough to touch. However, upon closer inspection, the neon sign appeared even more grimier.

Terri made a face. "Gotta theory on food poisoning?"

Clay chuckled, held the door, and followed behind. Together they experienced the pure shock of a downright seductive atmosphere.

"If looks could deceive . . ." Terri murmured stepping down into a large square dining room.

Robert Bromwell flinched.

Intimate high-backed booths lined the brick walls. In the center under a narrow shaft of light emanating from a ceiling spot, a lone guitar player hunched on a tall stool. Dressed in tight jeans, scuffed boots, and a Western shirt, he plucked chords at random.

"Must be more to Gingham than meets the eye," she commented, peeping around the menu at Clay. "I mean, who would of thought it'd be like this?"

Clay clasped his hand over hers. Slowly parting his lips, he was about to speak when haunting chords from the guitar player filled the room with magic. The old Western melody mystically mesmerized them.

Silverware clatter muted. Conversation ceased. Terri was barely aware of giving Clay carte blanche to order or the waitress slipping a plate in front of her. The grilled chicken could've been turnip greens.

At last she leaned back and sipped hot, hot coffee. The more the waitress poured, the more she drank. Gazing at Clay she tried to read his expression. Was he experiencing the same feelings that seemed to be building within her? She couldn't tell. The atmosphere was too . . . too relaxing. That's it. Relaxing. Keeping on the safe side she suggested they'd better leave for their big day tomorrow.

Before Clay could respond, the guitar player broke out into a rousing rendition of "You Are My Sunshine." The crowd came alive with singing. Clay couldn't resist. He had to join in. His Texas twang booming over the rest caught the attention of everyone. Several patrons came over to their booth to harmonize with him. On the last refrain, "Please don't take my sunshine away," he found her hand. Even in the darkened room she could see more in Clay's eyes than she wanted to acknowledge.

Slowly disengaging from his grasp, she took a small step toward the cashier station. Now was not the time to stray off course. Not now. Not when so much as at stake. Yet when Clay casually draped his arm around her shoulder, she was powerless to slip away from his touch.

Beside the boot sign, she murmured, "I need to leave a wake-up call."

Clay asked softly, "What time?"

"Five o'clock. I want to work Greenie before we leave." Her voice was barely audible.

Close to her, ear he breathed, "Why are we whispering?"

Terri's light, tinkling laughter matched the mood of her growing attraction to him. She couldn't stop smiling as they started on the walk across the parking lot. Strands from an old Merle Haggard love song wafted from the boot saloon across the desert sand producing a magical effect, goose fleshing her arms and lowering her protective feminine defenses.

At the door of Room 15 she scrambled in her shoulderbag for the key. Clay leaned toward her in a gentle manner. Facing him she sagged against the door. Somewhere along the way the funky glasses had disappeared, revealing a pair of luscious silver-gray eyes. Closing the gap, he took her face in his hands. His lips brushed the tip of her nose.

"Goodnight, Sunshine," he whispered, his breath rippling across her cheek. Shoving his hands in his pockets, he turned on his heel and started for Room 14.

"Clay?" she choked.

Glancing over his shoulder, he caught and held her

with smoky-gray eyes. His grin was so beautiful, she grinned back. Unaware of the full and sensuous tremble in her voice, she murmured, "See you in the morning."

Inside and still grinning, Terri took a deep breath. Clay had definitely taken on a new dimension, one she hadn't expected. Compared to Daryl Durand, he was decent to the core. She could just imagine what Daryl would have tried. She didn't care if Clay was an ex-drifter or not. That he had his own hauling business showed ambition. Work is work as long as it's honest.

Satisfied with her rationalization she went about the business of motel living, laying out clothes for the morning, leaving a wake-up call, brushing her teeth, and finally crawling into bed. Trying to snuggle under the stiff comforter, she silently cursed the amount of coffee she'd consumed. An hour passed.

The creak of Number 14's door jerked her upright. Pulling back the comforter she crept out of bed and to the window. Inching aside enough drape to expose one eye, she trained it on the pickup. Clay had his hand on the door handle. Must have forgotten something, she surmised. She couldn't move. She had to watch.

Glancing from side to side like a criminal on the lam, he eased open the driver's door and leaned over the front seat. Fascinated Terri spied on. The security light's glint made the metallic gold of the eyebrow pencil glow that he held in his hand. Her eyes bulged. Still she kept watching.

Fiddling under the driver's seat, he extracted the burgundy briefcase, the very one he'd denied bringing. In two steps he ducked backward through the door of Room 14. She heard it close behind him.

Reeling in astonishment, she let go of the drape. A sense of betrayal washed over her. He'd distinctly said he'd given the case to Rudd to give to Alfred. She'd assumed his partner would pick it up from Alfred. If he didn't want to use the case for Greenie's papers, why didn't he say so? What's he got in that briefcase anyway?

The questions burned and confused her thoughts to the point she couldn't make any sense why anyone would lie over such a trivial matter. Why couldn't he have admitted he didn't want to use his partner's case? No, he had to lie. Not a simple lie, either. An elaborate fabrication that involved Rudd and Alfred. If that wasn't enough, a twinge of jealousy sneaked in over the eyebrow pencil. Who did it belong to?

Coming to her senses, she tried counting the times she'd heard Clay say "trust me." Here she was stuck in the desert with Alfred's choice of an assistant, and how could she?

## Chapter Four

Terri shoved the last of her make-up articles deep in the bowels of her backpack and smoothed the velcro flap shut. She heard his footsteps. Bristling she waited for the knock.

Standing at attention, she commanded, "Enter."

"Morning, Sunshine."

His voice, soft and silvery, sent a ripple of awareness through her. Exercising restraint, she stared him down. "I am not your sunshine. Let's leave it at that. Okay?"

"Certainly. At your service."

"You don't have to salute," she grumbled.

"Do we eat before or after Greenie's work out?"

That he'd used the intimate name for Green Luck irritated her. Drained of patience, she enunciated with

all the authority she could muster, "After. That is today's schedule."

"My, my, my," he sang, picking up the luggage she
didn't get to first.

Arms full and without another word spoken, they
loaded the pickup. Relieved he was overly concentrating on driving, she stared straight ahead. *Why don't I
come right out and ask him about the briefcase? Why
don't I say if you didn't want to use it, why didn't you
say so? Why did you have to lie?* She paused, forcing
herself to calm down. Knowing Clay, he'd come back
with "how come you were spying on me?" A confrontation would ensue and strain the working relation-
ship they had to have. That was something she could
ill afford. Not with so much riding on the performance.
Grimly she decided to let it slide until she could talk
to Alfred or Rudd first. Modus operandi. Keep on
guard.

She checked the seat space separating them. Her
brain swirling half in anger, half in desperation, envi-
sioned an imaginary wall, a wall built on the arm rest
separating them. One she dared him to cross. In her
mind, she devised a blueprint. Instead of an equestrian
puissance wall built of hollow wooden blocks, she'd
build her's out of brick. That's it. Good solid brick, but
before she could get serious with the construction, she
felt obliged to give him one more chance. Reaching in
the door panel pocket, she removed Green Luck's papers and smoothed them across her lap.

"Too bad you left the case in Fresno," she said in a nonchalant manner. "I'd hate for any damage to come to these papers." Facing Clay head on, she held her breath.

"They'll be safe in the door pocket," he said.

She caught a muscle twitch in his jaw. A sure sign he's lying, she thought. In her mind she laid the first row of bricks on the space between them.

Interrupting her preoccupation Clay mentioned Team Win's approaching destination. He waited for a response. With none forthcoming, he flatly questioned, "What's the game plan?"

Terri cleared her throat. "Work Green Luck, walk him down, feed him in the trailer so he won't get *bored* traveling."

The dig wasn't lost on Clay. *Do I bore her? It's the pressure. Roy Scott is probably faring better. He's had the experience of both winning and losing big ones.* Glancing in her direction he checked her expression. He wished he could see her eyes, but her profile told him enough. Clamped jaws and tilted chin. He hated to see her so uptight.

As soon as he braked, Terri hopped from the truck and gave the trailer the once over. Relieved it was exactly as they had left it, she removed the working saddle and bridle from the tack compartment. When Clay offered to carry the saddle she marched away from him, bridle trailing from her shoulder. Stepping in front of her, he held up his palm like a traffic cop. She had no choice but to stop.

"Would you mind moving?" She gave him a steady glare.

"Team Win is a team. Now hand me the saddle." Light heartedly he added, "My mother taught me to be a gentleman."

"Oh? Really?" she scoffed. His mouth twitched and the devil flew in her. "Let's get something straight. I don't have to jump at your commands. Get it?"

"I got it. The saddle, please."

Exasperated, she tried side-stepping his imposing body. Now it was matter of principle. Not on her death bed would she relinquish the saddle. He kept in step with her. When she moved to the opposite side, he was there to block her.

"Shall we dance?" he quipped, bowing at the waist.

He had such an engaging grin she had to bite the inside of her cheek to keep a nervous giggle from escaping. Hanging on to the saddle she attempted a more-threatening glare.

"We're wasting time," she growled between her teeth. "You may have the saddle when we get to the stall."

"Does that mean I get to tack Green Luck?"

His teasing voice only added to her dilemma. "Only if you're lucky," she muttered under her breath.

"What was that?" He lightly tapped her arm.

She refused to answer. Her staccato march esca-
lated to a hard gallop. Clay merely lengthened his
stride to keep up. At Green Luck's stall and without
making eye contact she shoved the saddle into his
chest, squeezed open the stall door and slipped inside.

"I'll take him out," she said facing him through the
top half of the stall door. "I need a halter and a lead
line."

Clay clicked his heels. "Yes, ma'am."

With lightning speed he removed the tack from the
peg on the front of the stall and handed it to her.
"Anything else?"

She shook her head.

"What about a helmet?"

Terri knew *he* knew she'd forgotten it in her rush to
take charge of the saddle. "My fault," she admitted
jaws tight. "I'll get it."

When she returned, Clay was waiting with Green
Luck beside the fenced ring. Opening the gate for Clay
to lead Green Luck through she followed at a safe
distance behind. In the middle of the ring he halted,
swung the reins over the horse's head, and handed
them to Terri. Bracing herself for his leg up, she
mounted stiffly. With the repercussions of his touch
traveling up her leg she tucked her head and broke out
into a brisk trot.

In the distance she could see trail dust stirred by a
quarter horse's sliding stop. A cowboy with a cam-

corder on his shoulder caught the action. The stunt riders making a video, she thought. Then turning her mind on the task at hand she swallowed hard and let the years of equestrian training wash over her. The grueling courses in Ireland had gained Alfred's trust in her to bring home his final victory. She had to give it her best shot.

At one point she was vaguely aware of Clay suggestion that she take it easy. Still she went through the paces hard and fast. When she noticed lather gathering at the edge of the saddle pad she began to walk the horse.

Perspiration dripped from the sides of her safety helmet. On the fourth pass of walking down Green Luck, she unsnapped the strap and tossed the helmet over the fence at Clay. The unexpected movement caused the horse to stutter step sideways from the fence. Bending over the saddle she patted his sweat-drenched neck.

"That's a fair-sized horse," a ranch hand watching on the rail called out. "You look like a flea on his back."

She flashed him a grin. "I've heard worse!"

Clay had his hand on the gate. "Are you finished?"

She nodded.

Clay entered the ring, took the reins, and stood beside the horse. Swiftly she kicked the irons from her feet, swung her leg over the front of the saddle, and slid down the horse. The instant she touched ground, she began backing off. She saw the concern plainly registered in his eyes.

"Take a break," he said. "I need to cool down Greenie."

Terri joined Buckshot and several hands at the fence to watch Clay and Green Luck. Two of the hands turned out to be the stunt riders from Hollywood. With horse as the common denominator, Terri was in her element. She listened to their woes of having an agent who wanted film of them doing the impossible on horseback. The superficial camaraderie acted like a magnet to her. She participated, sometimes laughing a little too hard, until Clay approached her with the cooled-down horse.

Silently she and Clay sponged off Greenie, threw a sheet over him, and tied him inside the stall. While the horse dried, they gathered up supplies. Conscious of Clay's whereabouts at all times, she gave him a wide berth.

Before starting on the journey to the trailer, she couldn't resist saying so long to the little Shetland. The pony bared its teeth and pawed the bedding. Head wagging, she moved on.

"That was a tough work out you gave Green Luck," Clay commented in a safe matter-of-fact tone. "The horse has the stamina to go the course. I liked the way he worked off his backend. Lot of power there."

Bad as she hated to admit it, she respected his

observations. Rudd and Alfred echoed in them. Worried about the work out, though, as Clay had said, she didn't answer.

As soon as Green Luck was poised at the trailer ramp, she leaned inside the tack compartment for his feed. She could hear the clop-clop of the ascending hooves on the ramp followed by the flat-footed clump-clump of the horse crossing the rubber stall mat. Through the metal partitions of the compartment, Greenie's throat rumblings echoed.

She ducked out the trailer. Handing the bucket of grain to Clay, she said, "He's earned his oats. Do you mind?"

He gave an audible sigh. Standing beside the trailer he opened the small door at Greenie's head and dumped the grain on the shelf under the horse's nose. "See?" he reminded her. "You do need me."

"I could have climbed up on the trailer fender and fed him myself. Is the hay bag full?"

"You bet."

Terri started for the cab door.

Taking her by the shoulders he turned her around. "For you, for Alfred, and for Green Luck we have to be a team and trust each other to do their job," he said in an odd, but gentle, tone.

Yanking free from him, she frowned at him with a glaze of despair spreading across her face. "What do you think I've been trying to tell you?"

*Gaby Pratt*

Watching her backside climb into the cab, he resisted climbing in after her. He wanted to hold her until the anguish in her eyes subsided. The barrier growing between them was disturbing. He had to take action, careful action, but action.

## Chapter Five

"Let's try communication," Clay suggested waiting to pull out on Route 40.

Terri blinked. Communication? He's a fine one to mention communication. Twisting in the seat, she stewed. He was right. Think team. Too much was at stake. She knew that. It brought her to her senses.

"Any suggestions?"

Wiping her sunglasses with a tissue, she said, "Here's one. Why don't you get a pair a clip-on shades? I mean, I don't see how you stand the glare." From the depths of her shoulderbag, she pulled up a second pair of sunglasses. "Can you use these?"

"Nope. Need my own."

Drumming her fingers across the bag she finally

63

tossed it over her shoulder and onto the back bench. Again the pills rattled in their bottles.

"Did you take your vitamins this morning?" he asked, genuinely interested.

*Communication is good.* "Sure did. Tough though. The water in the motel tasted like pond scum. You never did tell me how you met Alfred."

Clay flexed his grip on the steering wheel. "We go back a long way."

*Here we go again.* "How long?"

"Years ago Alfred did a tremendous favor for me." His voice ended in a note discouraging further pursuit.

Undaunted, Terri kept at it. "What kind of favor?"

"Let's just say it's personal." To lessen his brusque reply, he added, "Alfred called me three weeks ago to schedule this trip. I was flattered he'd asked. As we all know this event is very important to him."

Terri twisted in the seat for a full view of Clay. "Did he tell you about the showdown then? I mean, you knew more about it before I did. Even before Rudd."

"After the initial phone call, I talked to Alfred daily to negotiate details. He impressed on me how no foul-ups would be tolerated. In his mind he had to be confident I could handle any situation that might arise."

*Now he sounds like a lawyer.* "As secretive as Alfred is, it seems funny he would share so much information."

Clay chuckled. "He made me swear to secrecy. Remember that. This old Texas boy took an oath."

He's joking, she thought. "I bet Cora Stuart is freaking out. She doesn't have a clue what she's up against."

"In her boots I'd freak." Clay agreed.

Terri nodded. "You don't pull a grand prix horse and rider out of thin air . . . unless you're Alfred McDonnell."

"Your turn. How did you meet our eccentric boss?" Clay changed lanes to make room for a stock trailer to pass.

Terri leaned forward to get a better view of the cows. "Long story."

The load of cattle rattled by.

"We've got time."

"I met Alfred at Bennington Stables. One night I was by myself. The entire staff, boarders, everybody had gone to a show. Alfred stopped by to check a mare for sale. I knew who he was, but it didn't matter. I made him as comfortable as I could, and asked him to wait until I finished feeding. Well, he wasn't about to sit. He followed me around, watched everything I did, and asked a million questions. I'll never forget it."

"How long ago was that?"

Terri hesitated. "Four, no, five years ago. Alfred kept coming back to scope the mare, but he ended up hiring me." The pride in her voice gushed. "That's the break to die for."

Clay's brief gaze like light caught in water connected with her. "What happened next?"

Terri drew her lips in a tight smile. "He sent me and Greenie to Ireland for training. Haggarty Farms to be exact. Alfred has a connection with the owner. I have to tell you, Green Luck liked to not have made it back. He suffered a colic attack over the Atlantic, no place to walk him down, it was awful."

"I know." Clay smiled.

Terri's eyes popped. "How? I mean Alfred kept that close to his vest. Who told you?"

He swallowed a dry lump. "There's no space in an aircraft cargo area to handle a horse. The stalls are tight."

Terri began to worry. Maybe she shouldn't have mentioned it. "Rudd took over when we got back and nearly killed me with his training. He never slacked off."

"He's tough all right," Clay commented.

Grinning, she bobbed her chin. "Paid off though."

"What was his training like?"

"If you're looking for any training secrets, forget it," she replied testily.

"No . . . no, that's not what I meant."

She paused to gather her thoughts. "Rudd says you either have it or you don't. There's no way to teach split-second decisions, timing, reflexes, or how to work under pressure. Practice, he says, and determination helps build on the talent you have. The best advice he ever gave me was save something for the last fence."

"How do you accomplish that?"

"This is the plain and simple truth. Honesty is everything, and this is as honest as I can be." She paused, twisted in the seat, and looked him straight in the eye. "Rudd says ice water flows in my veins."

Clay grinned. "Tough to the grainy marrow of your bones."

If he took the honesty hint, his reply didn't reveal it. "Suggestion two, tell me your background." In the same breath she tacked on, "I want details."

"I grew up outside of Dallas."

"Details, please."

"We had a few horses, cows, and a couple of acres. Mom liked to groom horses, Dad dreamed of breeding the perfect Quarter Horse. His passion was bull riding."

She couldn't help noticing how carefully he'd selected his words. Is he telling the truth? How did he end up being a drifter? She plowed on. "Did he rodeo?"

"Nope. Spectator only."

The clicking turn signal ended the conversation. Bearing down on the stock trailer, he passed the rig with ease. After a few miles of silence, he asked if she were hungry.

"I worked Greenie pretty hard this morning. The quicker we get to Flagstaff, the happier I'll be. I mean, I don't want him cooped up in the trailer any longer than he has to be. Let's make a fast pit stop."

"Good idea. Suggestion three." Joggling her knee he touched the callous built up by years of gripping a horse on the inside of her knee. "Think Team Win."

The sudden physical intimacy got her attention. For her own protection she added a few more rows of bricks to the imaginary wall. High enough to pass his silver belt buckle.

Clay pulled in the parking area fronting a mini-market and service pumps. He'd barely braked before Terri was out of the cab and at the little door beside Greenie's head. Climbing up on the fender she reached over and unlatched it.

A magnificent gray head burst through the opening. Ears pricked, nostrils flared, he fixed a stare beyond Terri. Over her shoulder she saw the object of Green Luck's attention. A little girl in a T-shirt with a dancing Kachina across the front watched in awe. Her ebony black braids matched her inquisitive button eyes.

Ogling Green luck, the youngster stepped forward. "Is he a rodeo horse?"

Smiling, Terri shook her head. "No. He jumps big fences."

Catching the disappointment on the child's face she began digging in her canvas bag. "Here we go," she said, handing her a McDonnell Stables business card. On the front was a picture of a grand prix horse and rider midway a vertical fence. "This is what he does."

"Wow!" She gazed up at Terri.

"You can have the card. The address of where I work is on the back."

Clay joined in. "The first of the week this horse will be in an event in Fiddle, Texas. It'll be on the Rodeo Channel."

"Thanks," the little girl exclaimed. With stars in her eyes, she ran to show the treasure to her parents.

Terri watched as the family headed toward a blue pickup loaded with welding equipment. At the last minute, the little girl turned and waved. Wrapped in her own thoughts, Terri started for the mini-market. Silently, Clay walked by her side.

Inside the market, she pointed out the rack of sunglasses before wandering over to the coffeepot on the end of the deli table. While she filled a large cup, Clay came up beside her. Conscious of his attempt to divert her attention from the pastries to wheat muffins, the muffins he'd chosen for himself, she elbowed him off.

Not waiting for him, she took off for the cashier station. On the counter a basket of bananas caught her eye. She turned to point out the fruit to Clay.

Not only had he purchased clip-ons, but the pop-up kind as well. At the precise moment of eye contact he'd flipped up the orange disks, widened his eyes, and made a buzzing sound. Imitating a nerdy bumblebee, he gave it all he had. Moving close to her, he dipped his head against her neck and buzzed in her ear. Giggling and slapping at his head, she turned and faced him. So close together she was captivated by the change in his eyes. Eyes that communicated things she didn't want to think about. Determined not to crumble she reached up, flipped the disks down, gathered her purchases, and marched stiffly out the door.

At the trailer Clay tapped Green Luck's nose until the horse withdrew enough for him to latch the little door. Next he pulled the rig to the pumps. Perfect, thought Terri and excused herself. She said she'd forgotten gum. Not only did she purchase gum, but six candy bars as well. Feeling downright proud of herself, she stuffed them in her bag.

Back in the cab she dropped the gum in the door pocket, turned to Clay, and smiled sweetly. At last— with all seatbelts fastened and a final check through the rearview mirror—the emerald-green Dodge and the jet-black trailer pulled out on Route 40. Destination: Flagstaff.

Taking a bite of pastry, Terri wondered if he'd mention her diet. Wrinkling her brow she figured he'd given up on her sugar intake. "What about RDB? Doesn't he drive too?"

"RDB?" Clay repeated.

Exasperated, she frowned. Her voice took on an edge. "The one the briefcase belongs to. You know the one you gave Rudd to give to Alfred."

"Yes, he drives sometimes. In fact", he added, trying to make eye contact with her, "I wish he'd taken this assignment instead of me."

"Oh, really?" Despite best intentions her voice caught.

"Terri," he said in desperation. "Look at me."

"Why?" Staring straight ahead, she wouldn't budge in his direction no matter what.

"I know I'm not handling this right. You're under so much pressure I don't want to add to it. Believe me that's last thing I want to do."

Terri refused to so much as blink.

Gripping the steering wheel he muttered more to himself than to Terri, "I could strangle Alfred McDonnell."

"Leave Alfred out of it!" Shocked by the forcefulness of her voice, she hugged herself and glared at the passing scenery. The yellows, tans, and beiges of the mountainous formations that'd erupted from the earth millions of years ago contrasted the purple-blue sky. *How dare he question Alfred.*

To keep on track, she methodically began listing every piece of tack used by Green Luck. Next she mentally dressed herself in white breeches, black hunt coat, and cap. In her mind she imagined the friends and admirers of Alfred's, old cronies of Cora's, Jake Bob Johnson's curious staff, and the media. Without Rudd on hand to walk the course, Alfred's comments would be invaluable.

Lastly she put Clay into the picture. He'd hand her

a crop, tighten the girth, and adjust Greenie's bridle. From the height of the horse, she would look down at Alfred and Clay. From past experience, she'd detect a competitor's glint in Alfred's eyes. What would Clay do? Give her a thumbs up? Make a joke?

Faced with the hard truth concerning Clay Moore, she took a deep breath. Like it, or not, Clay, per Alfred McDonnell, was part of the picture. Just because he made her laugh and caused her senses to tingle was inconsequential. Yes, she would keep the wall between them unless it concerned Green Luck. Now, how hard is that? she asked herself. Glancing at the gray upholstery separating them, she added another row of bricks.

"Clay," she began her chin tucked, eyes focused on the dashboard. "No more remarks about Alfred. This . . . this was sort of sprung on me."

"I understand," he said, his voice heartfelt. "Forgive me."

Terri examined her fingernails before she looked at him. Immediately he straightened in the seat and pretended to adjust a necktie. He licked the palm of his hand and slicked back his hair. Next came the operatic warm-up. At last he spoke like a swearing-in officer of the court.

"I hereby promise never again to express a disparaging remark no matter how well-intended about Alfred McDonnell so long as we both shall live."

Terri's tinkling laughter filled the cab. "Should I say amen?"

"All together now, one, two, three . . ."

In unison they solemnly pledged amen.

Picking up the conversation, Clay remarked, "Your little fan was Navajo, I bet. Their tribe is big on extended families."

She felt safe with the subject of Navajos. "That little girl was her father's clone."

He glanced at her. "Are you your father's clone?"

Terri knew it was an innocent question. She couldn't, wouldn't deny the facts. "Last I heard he was in Florida on a fishing boat. That is, if he's not drunk."

Clay made a move to touch her knee. She saw it coming and gave him a bodies-off-bounds expression. Withdrawing his hand from mid-air, he replaced it on the steering wheel. "That must have been hard on your mother."

"Bette, my grandma, raised me," she said softly.

Clay wanted to ask more, but her tone warded him off. Her vulnerability and her honesty touched him. He wanted her in his arms. More than anything he wanted to confess about his own father. He went to the local rodeos all right. Not only as a spectator, but as the town's one and only medical doctor to lend a hand to the injured riders. There were always injured riders.

He wanted to tell her about the night he decided not to follow in his father's footsteps. The night Cory was hooked, thrown in the air, and landed on his neck. He was just a kid, nineteen, and his neighbor. His death brought untold devastation to Cory's relatives and, right then and there, he knew he'd have problems keeping a professional distance from grieving families. Instead he became a dedicated veterinarian. For the first time he wanted to share what brought on his career decision and he couldn't. He couldn't even tell her his name.

"Radio?" he choked, faking a dry cough.

Terri shrugged. Even so she wasn't prepared for the lyrics leaping out at her ". . . alibis . . . lying eyes . . . cheated on . . ." Figuring it was either an omen or a reality check, she added another row of bricks.

Clay hummed along. She retreated into her own cocoon. When her body became sore in one position, she shifted to another. So many disturbing doubts crowded her thoughts about Clay Moore. *Haven't I learned anything? The truth, plain and simple, is all I ask.*

"FYI," Clay said, weariness in to his voice, "the out-of-favor team member is closing in on the horse motel."

"What do you mean out-of-favor?" she challenged.

"We're shutting each other out, Terri. That's not good. Not good for team players."

"Hey, I'm doing my part. What about you?"

"Best I can under the circumstances," he said in a tone begging for understanding.

Approaching the front entrance of the horse motel,

Terri came alive. The tree-lined dirt lane ended in front of a metal deluxe-prefabricated stable with a fenced paddock of white pipe. The stable door was wide open, and she could see the stalls inside. A snappy little tractor hauling a load of alfalfa pulled up beside the truck. Before Clay cut the motor she pushed the electric window button and hung her head outside.

"Howdy," the driver called up to her. "You must be from McDonnell Stables. Be right with you."

Tasting the dry earth kicked up by the tractor and so at home in a horse complex she almost offered to help.

Clay called from the rear of the trailer, "Can you check Green Luck before I let down the ramp?"

She climbed the fender and peeked inside the little window. Her stomach growled. Visions of steak, baked potato, sour cream—lots of sour cream—crossed her mind. Mouth salivating, she checked the lead line fastened to the halter.

"Okay . . . fine!" she sang out.

Greenie, shifting weight, slightly rocked the trailer. The ramp thudded to the ground. On her way to the rear of the rig she heard Greenie's hoof rake the boarded incline. At the edge of the trailer, she stopped cold. The uneasy look on Clay's face set off an alarm.

Stumbling, disoriented, the horse swung his elegant head around to nip at his side. Running to the distressed animal, she took Greenie's face in both hands and stared at the agony in the purple velvet eyes.

"Clay. We have a problem." Her voice shook.

"Get on the other side," he instructed. "We'll walk him around. Be careful."

A cry of fright escaped her lips. Frozen, she watched Green Luck's knees buckle as the horse started to go down.

## Chapter Six

Alfred relaxed in his favorite chair watching a mute weatherman point to a map. Better not conk out, he mused. It's time for Robert to call in. Fiddling around in his shirt pocket, he found the aid and shoved it in place. The television noise startled him. "Dadburn remote controls," he muttered, searching for the off button.

His orange cats—one fat, the other sassy—joined him in the chair. Honey curled up in his lap. Poised at attention Diablo held down the chair arm.

*Brrrring.*

Diablo hissed. Honey kneaded his thigh.

"This is Zina Cook," the voice chirped. "May I speak to Alfred McDonnell?"

Recognizing the caller, he grumbled, "Speaking."

"I'm from the *Equestrian Herald*. I'd like to confirm a rumor about a shoot-out between you and Cora Stuart."

Alfred grunted.

Trying a different tactic, she cheerfully continued, "Would you care to make a comment?"

"No comment," he said, his voice a snarl.

"Your secrecy is legendary," Zina cajoled. "My editors will agree to an appointment any place, anytime."

Alfred remained silent.

"Pictures?" she asked hopefully.

Alfred snorted. "No comment or pictures at this time."

"Is the shoot-out for real? Can you answer that?"

Alfred shifted in the chair. "Not interested in any interview. Bye now." He hung up.

Settling back he let his thoughts wander. He knew he was secretive. He didn't need to be prodded by some pip-squeak. He also knew it worked. On the show grounds his cardinal rule for McDonnell Stables was keep your plans to yourself. If they pan out, great. If not, no backpedaling necessary. In the meantime, the competition worries.

He chuckled to himself. Funny how his reputation got started. How many years ago? My Alice took the mare . . . what was her name? Frustrated, he wrinkled his brow. Seconds later Silverkiss popped up in his brain. Silverkiss. How could he forget that?

Alice believed in Kissy. Not convinced the horse was ready, he remembered plotting with her. We'll show up and be quiet. If the mare does well we'll pretend we'd planned it that way. If she doesn't we won't have to justify anything. We'll say we're schooling her. His eyes watered at the remembrance of the announcer calling out the winner, Silverkiss, owned by McDonnell Stables, shown by Alice McDonnell. Her endearing smile, the smile of a winner, was indelibly etched on his heart.

That became their policy. Arrive quietly, show bravely, and bring home the championship. Over the years the strategy developed into a style associated with his stables. So closely tied with Alice and the mare he refused to discuss it, which compounded his reputation. Not many people were left who even remembered he was briefly married. Two years and two days to be exact. The sole redemption of the cruel disease was she didn't suffer long.

Fidgeting with the Honey's silky ears he regretted dismissing Henry, his housekeeper, cook, and master of all trades, for the night. He could've engaged him in a hand of poker to pass the time. Down to a staff of one, he wondered where the years had gone. Startled by the chiming doorbell, he rose from the chair, dumping the cat in the process.

Surprised to find his attorney and equestrian confidant, Martin Riggs, he warmly greeted his old friend. Martin's florid complexion and silver hair was accentuated by his suit, shirt, and tie, all in variegated shades of gray.

"What brings you out this time of night?"

"I was on my way home," Martin replied. "I stopped by on the chance you'd be free to discuss the future of the stables." Glancing around, he asked, "Where's Henry?"

"He's retired for the night." Alfred started in the direction of the great room. Martin followed.

Seated in a dark-cherry velvet wing-back chair opposite Alfred, Martin placed his briefcase on his knees, unzipped it, and began shuffling papers. Frowning, Alfred observed the action. It was as if the pages Martin ruffled were the pages of his life. Tonight he wasn't in the mood to think about what lay ahead. He'd rather talk about the showdown.

He wanted to share the suspense with his trusted friend to ward off the melancholy seeping into his bones. Curious of Martin's reaction about Robert's disguise, he sorely regretted the oath of silence. For Robert to be incognito was classic. It'd be talked about on the show circuit long after he was gone.

"I'm waiting on Rob . . ." Alfred coughed trying to recall the masked-rider's name. "Terri," he substituted, "to check in. They should be in Flagstaff by now."

"I'll have to hand it to you. You and Cora came up with one heck of a way to decide once and for all who has the best horse. Does anyone know your plans for afterwards?"

"Not yet. You are flying out with me, aren't you?"

"I wouldn't miss it for the world. We'll have to leave

early. Airport security is time-consuming." Crossing the space between them, Martin handed him a sheaf of papers. "Here are the copies of the reports you wanted. Do you have any contingency plans in case the showdown results aren't in your favor?"

Alfred gave a snort. "What do you mean? That's not an option. The Luck's in better form than Bewick Swan. The Swan's slowing down."

"Slowing down? I don't believe it. With Roy Scott in the irons that horse can fly."

Alfred edged forward, his voice conspiratorial. "Between you, me, and the fence post, Doc Bromwell says the horse is passing its prime. He scoped him at the Nationals. The Swan still wins, but he won't against Green Luck."

"Robert Bromwell!" Martin exclaimed. "When did you talk to him? I've been trying to reach him all week."

Rubbing his chin, Alfred mumbled, "Not too long ago. What do you need him for?"

"Clients of mine swear they've been cheated on a frozen semen deal. Artificial insemination case. They're out a ton of money, and I wanted Robert's opinion on it."

"He's pretty sharp," Alfred commented.

"I agree, but what's disturbing is not one soul in his office will give a clue as to where he is. I even called New Bolton Center at the University of Pennsylvania."

"Maybe he's gone fishing," Alfred offered.

"Robert has never taken a vacation as long as I've known him." Thoughtfully he questioned, "Bewick Swan slowing down? Do you think Cora's aware?"

"Probably not. She's too close to the horse."

"Speaking of the showdown, what about this hauler?" Pulling out two sheets of computer paper from the briefcase he began to read off the top. "Clay Moore, Equine Transportation. He's included a list of destinations, approximate arrival and departures times, and dates. At the bottom it says Texas-based, no address, no phone number, nothing." Puzzled, he looked to Alfred.

Alfred conjured up a blank expression. "His address might be in the Rolodex on my desk at the stable. Did you check with my secretary at the main office?"

"Standard procedure, Alfred. Where did Clay Moore come from? He's not anyone you've used before."

Alfred veered from a blank look to hardcore stonewalling. "He's a great hand with horses and an excellent driver. Can't spare any of the staff at this time," he said, knowing his tone would squelch further inquiries.

Martin sighed tucking the papers back in the case. "I guess we'll get the information when he bills us."

Alfred grunted.

"What about Green Luck? Think he's had enough experience? The puissance wall, of all things."

"I don't anticipate any problem. Terri and the Luck

have a special bond of trust and communication. That combination doesn't come along too often."

"That's true," Martin agreed. "I've seen Rudd put her through the paces. She and that horse are poetry in motion."

Drifting off into a world of his own, Alfred smiled.

Martin zippered the briefcase. Rising from the wing-back chair, he said, "I'll begin notifying the appropriate authorities concerning the stables tomorrow, if you approve."

"Hold off proceedings until the middle of next week. I'd like to get the showdown settled first. I'm not going to change my mind, Martin. It's just that I don't want another host of rumors started. The *Herald* has already called."

"I'm not going to ask what you told Zina."

"Not one blasted thing!" Alfred exclaimed vigorously.

Martin laughed. "I knew it. Are you sure you want to go through with this? The future of the stables will be final."

"I told you before," Alfred said slightly agitated. "When my body can't keep up I want out."

At the door saying good night, Martin half-jokingly asked, "You're not sick, are you?"

"Heck, no. Doc says I'm fine, but what does he know? I rode that chestnut mare . . . you know, the one in the end stall two months ago and I've still got a hitch to my gait."

Martin Rigg's eyes widened. "Was Rudd around?"

"Indeed, he was. I thought his ticker was going to give out on him."

Martin appeared uneasy. "Take care," he said.

Dousing lights as he passed, Alfred made his way down the hall and back to the great room. At the fireplace, he paused. Like so many times before he gazed at the portrait of Alice above the mantel. His eyes misted. Her smile had started so much. It was only fitting to end with one.

He slumped in the chair. The light from the table lamp splashed a pale-yellow glow over the cell phone charger anchored at the base. Shadowed in darkness the room seemed to envelope him. Honey found his lap. Stroking the cat, he began to worry what was going on.

## Chapter Seven

Terri grabbed the halter. The momentum of the horse going down was too much. She moved to the opposite side. In sync with Clay they hooked their shoulders under Greenie's and shoved with all their might. She broke out in a sweat. Clay grunted. After a hard desperate push, Greenie scrambled his legs under him. Weight on all fours the horse shivered, showed the white of his eyes.

"We've got to keep him up and moving," Clay said, tossing her the lead line.

Terri caught the nylon rope. "Come on, Greenie."

The horse took a few tentative steps.

"Hold it," Clay called out.

Looking over her shoulder, she watched him angling himself behind the horse to monitor its respiration by the rise and fall of the flanks. Next he placed his ear against the horse's side. When he asked for the thermometer and the scope, she took off without question. Colic screamed in her brain. A vision of Green Luck going down, his intestines twisting, a final throat rumble tormented her mind.

Clammy, shaky fingers held back the tail for Clay to insert the thermometer. An eternity passed. At last he removed the thermometer, held it at eye level, and turned it until he could read the numbers. She held her breath until he announced it normal, a good sign.

Placing the ends of the stethoscope in his ears, he winked at her. She couldn't keep her eyes off him. There was something about his movements, the way he listened to Greenie's gut rumblings, that was professional. She'd seen it done enough to know the difference. An unexpected surge of confidence in him flowed through her.

Smiling, he tried to tuck the scope in a lab coat pocket that wasn't there. Embarrassed he handed the instrument to her. "He'll be okay as long as we keep him on his feet."

"We need a vet," she said, her voice firm.

"I think it'll pass. Come on. Let's walk him."

She gasped. "What if something happens?"

"It's more important to walk him than to try and track down a vet. Let's get moving."

In her heart she knew Alfred and Rudd would have said the same thing.

At the corner of the fenced paddock area they met up with the proprietor. He introduced himself as Spencer Harvick. Right off the bat he asked if this was the horse headed for Jake Bob's arena and a blowout with Cora Stuart.

Terri sucked in. "News travels fast."

Harvick laughed. Instead of elaborating on where he got his information, he focused his attention on Green Luck. "I saw you unloading him. Got a problem?"

Clay took over. "A mild touch of colic. Under the circumstances we'll be spending the night on the premises. Is that okay with you?"

"Sure. Don't blame you one bit," he replied graciously. "There's a bathroom and shower next to the wash stall. Feel free, but let me warn you. If you use the shower use the can of foot powder on the shelf too."

Clay grinned. "Thanks for the tip."

"Put the horse in the end stall, keep the lights on if you like. In other words make yourself at home."

Terri spoke up. "What about a vet just in case?"

"Her number is on the blackboard in the tack room. She's pretty good about coming out. If I can be of anymore help track me down. Trail riders are coming in, and I need to finish putting up a load of hay."

When he was safely out of hearing distance, Terri said, "That goes to show you how fast news travels on the horse circuit. If a facility in the middle of Arizona knows about the showdown, so does everybody else."

Before Clay could answer Green Luck nipped at his side.

They walked around the stables, beside the pipe fence and down a path. Periodically Clay stopped, checked Greenie. After a half hour of keeping the horse from rolling, recovery seemed to be spontaneously taking care of itself. The sweat on Robert's brow ceased. Periodically, Terri had held her breath. Both sighed simultaneously.

When the first star sparkled they leaned against the pipe fence. The horse had remained quiet for over an hour.

"Think it's safe to bring him in and feed him?" Terri asked rubbing the back of her neck.

Yawning, Clay stretched. "You bet."

His slow answer caused Terri to frown. "Are you sure?"

He nodded. "Now that we've stopped, I don't want to move. I can't remember the last time I watched the stars come out." Shuffling around Greenie to Terri's side he slipped his arm around her waist. "Come on," he said, his voice deep and pulsating. "It's been a long day."

After wrestling Green Luck with Clay, she told herself they'd bonded together with the horse and that made it all right to lean against him just a little on the trek back to the stable. Clip-clopping behind, Green Luck gave a snort.

The routine of hauling supplies and feed from the truck went smoothly. A nod or a slight murmur was the only communication necessary. When the last chore was finished, Clay draped his arms across Greenie's back. Leaning his body against the horse, he buried his face between his elbows.

"Look," he said, making eye contact with her from under one arm. "I'm moving the truck to the side of the stables under Green Luck's window. We'll be able to hear if he starts to go down again."

"I'll call Alfred. He needs to know. If I can't get him on the cell phone, I'll try the one in his office."

Clay dug the palms of his hands in his eye sockets. Sighing, he pulled back his shoulders, rotated his head. "Tell him a mild, very mild, touch of colic." As she turned to leave, he corrected himself. "No, don't say colic. Tell him a slight discomfort. He'll want to know it was probably triggered by something in the desert water."

*I should have thought of that*, she fumed. *After all, I did drink the stuff when I took the vitamins. Now he sounds like a vet.* Fumbling in her bag for the phone, she found herself wording a conversation to Alfred which would be the least alarming. At the same time she couldn't shake the closeness she felt toward Clay until her brain niggled an odd reminder, the eyebrow pencil. Punching in Alfred's numbers in the middle of Flagstaff was no time to be thinking thoughts best left alone.

Alfred answered on the second ring. She put the best spin possible on the situation, but when she said "a slight discomfort" Alfred's bark rattled her eardrums.

"Let me speak to Robert," he demanded.

"Robert?" Terri repeated. She could hear Clay bounding toward her. "Er, Alfred—"

Grabbing the phone from her hand, Clay lightly shoved her aside. Dumbfounded she was about to protest, but it was too late. He had Alfred's attention. She tapped the toe of her right boot.

"It's Clay," he said raking his long fingers through his hair. "Not Robert."

Terri tapped her toe harder. The rubber mat covering the tack room floor muffled the thump, thump, thump. During Clay's entire report she thumped. Once he caught her eye and pleaded for understanding. She wasn't buying it. At last he told Alfred goodnight and hung up.

Before she could speak, he reached out for her and took her shoulders in his hands. His eyes were so full of repentance, she was momentarily paralyzed.

"Sorry, I grabbed the phone," he apologized, gently squeezing her shoulders. "Please forgive me."

Back against the tack room wall she felt trapped and hurt. Words stuck in her throat. Her voice quivered. "Why, Clay? Why did you do that?"

"I knew Alfred had me mixed up with Robert . . . my partner. The last thing I wanted to do was confuse him."

"R—RDB," she sputtered, bristling with indignation. "The one the briefcase belongs to."

He regarded her quizzically for a moment. "Yes."

She stepped out of his arms. Vowing one day to get to the bottom of the briefcase, she said, skepticism in her voice, "Thank you for the explanation. I'm grateful for any *explanation* you care to share."

"You're welcome." Playfully he touched her nose with his fingertip. "Hey, I said I'm sorry. Let's go to the truck. It's going to be a long night."

She knew he expected her to follow him. Instead she remained glued to the floor mat staring at his backside angling through the door. Taking a deep breath, she rubbed her nose. With her heart in her throat and a million questions on her mind, she marched out the door.

While Clay put away the last of Greenie's supplies, she climbed in the truck. Grateful for the horse sheet, clean but still smelling of horse, he'd spread out for her. Glancing at the space between herself and the driver's seat, she made sure the wall, her own puissance wall was in place and the imaginary bricks were solidly stacked. Satisfied she reclined the seat, scrunched around and ended up stretched out straight, her arms folded across her chest. When Clay poked his head in the window, she came forward.

"Are you decent?" he asked, wiggling both brows at her.

Frustrated she blurted, "Get in the blasted truck."

Going out of his way to be perfectly quiet opening the door he eased inside. Each movement he made was slow, calculated, and soundless. She couldn't stand the suspense and stole a peek.

"I think we should go over the game plan," she said. "I'll keep a check on Greenie. You sleep. I can sleep on the road tomorrow."

"We can both take turns," he said good-naturedly. "With the windows open we can hear if he starts to go down."

Turning her back on him she focused on the moonlight glinting off the silver door handle. Her stomach growled. Suddenly her eyes widened. A smile spread across her face.

Ever so daintily, she asked, "Are you hungry?"

"Starved," he replied. "Be brave. We can make it."

"You can be brave," she taunted. "I have candy bars."

Clay shot up. "Candy bars!"

"Relax," she said, making no effort to hide the smugness in her voice. "I've got six of them."

Rubbing his hands together, he grinned at her.

Wasting no time she fished around in her canvas bag, pulled up a chocolate bar and was about to toss it to him. She drew back her hand. "Too bad," she gibed with a sigh. "This will jitter your nerves. Sorry. Think Team Win."

"Did I ever tell you my theory of jitters versus starvation?"

"No, I don't believe you have." She started to toss the bar and again drew back. She placed the back of her hand against her forehead. "Oh, oh, think of your poor muscles. The sugar will draw water from them, such a pity. I don't sign up with teams that don't respect their muscles."

His deep, warm laughter filled the cab. "Here," she said, stifling her own giggles. "Live dangerously." The bar landed on his sleeve.

At the first rustle of hay and paw of Greenie's hoof audible through the opened windows, Terri was out the truck and running. Pulling back the stall door, she eased inside. Clay was directly behind her.

Greenie, nose deep in the feeder, slowly swung his head in her direction. At the same time Clay took a step forward and placed his hands on her shoulders. His thumbs rested at the base of her neck. Sandwiched between the horse and Clay, she felt a sense of entrapment that brought forth both comfort and uncertainty. The touch of his thumb position bothered her.

"He's okay. Just putting away groceries," she said, knowing Clay was smiling. His hands on her shoulders had a way of communicating to her. When he applied pressure to her neck muscle with his thumbs, she felt the tension drain from her body. It was difficult to remain standing. Executing pure grit, she slipped from his grasp. Pivoting on her heel, she peered up at him and muttered, "False alarm. Let's go back to bed."

His devilish grin was back. "Best idea we've had yet."

Terri blushed. "Let me rephrase that."

Back in the cab she pulled the ends of Greenie's

sheet around her. Settling in her cocoon she listened
to Clay shift, groan, and curse the sheet strap wrapped
around his ankle. When not the slightest movement
was left to be made, he spoke up.

"Goodnight, Sunshine."

"Goodnight, Alfred McDonnell's choice of assistant."

Terri dozed off, but it was an uneasy kind of doze.
Her mind waffled between the effect Clay was having
on her and Green Luck's belly ache. Finally she
eased out the truck.

The Luck appeared to be content, not in any pain.
"Good grief," she told the horse. "I'm getting as bad
as Rudd fussing over you like a mother hen, but we
have so much riding on this venture." She tugged its
forelock, patted its neck. "Do you understand?"

Walt Disney would have said the horse nodded yes,
but she knew better. He was just being a horse. The
problem was it was Alfred's horse. What if she messed
up? What if she let everybody down? Never mind if
she did her best, Green Luck did his. They had to win.

Taking pains not to make any noise, she climbed
back in the truck. Clay had his arm draped across his
eyes. In a quiet voice, he asked, "How's he doing?"

"No droppings. His water bucket is almost full." Her
voice had a catch to it. A sniff followed. Wadding herself up in the horse sheet, she turned her back on him.
Tears of pure, unadulterated worry gathered and began
to spill down her cheeks.

Clay sat up. Leaning over he gathered her in his arms. "Hey, now," he whispered. "It's not that bad. Greenie's going to be all right. I guarantee it."

Cradled in his arms, she knew she should back off. The comfort, the security, the concern was hard to resist. *I'll push him away in a minute*, she told herself. One minute won't hurt.

Terri blinked awake. Squinting she could make out the side of the stable from Clay's window. Still in his arms she was astonished at the position of her knee in his lap.

Backing off, she sat up. Clay didn't move. His even breathing signaled she hadn't disturbed his sleep. About to slip out the truck, she glimpsed the dark-framed glasses resting on the very spot she'd built her imaginary wall.

Flipping up the orange disks she held the lenses to her eyes. Puzzled, she frowned. Peering through the glasses again she came to an alarming conclusion. *These lenses are plain. No prescription.*

Slowly she turned the frames over in her hand and read the smeared inscription engraved in imitation gold on the ear piece: Hally Trick, Inc. Folding the frames carefully she placed them on the dashboard. Turning back to Clay she stared at his boldly handsome face. Ever so desperately she tried to grasp the meaning of the fake glasses. When he stirred she slipped out the cab.

## Chapter Eight

Clay couldn't stop grinning. Pulling out on Route 40 headed for Albuquerque, he simply couldn't stop. His jaws ached from it. If Alfred had told him he'd fall for his rider, he wouldn't have believed it. He worried though. How old is she? Twenty-five? Twenty-seven max. *Will she think I'm too old for her? Is she the youth I missed keeping my nose to the grind?* Come on, he reprimanded himself. Matters of the heart are ageless. At least, he hoped so.

Ever since the onslaught of notoriety over his colic procedure, horse people hounded him on sight for his opinion. Attending the Nationals for Alfred was a wake-up call. He could imagine a repeat at Jake Bob's. He knew they'd have their hands full dealing with the pressure of the Super Bowl.

"Got your pop-ups in place?" she growled.

"Yes, ma'am."

"What's wrong with your eyes anyway?"

Her tone pricked his guilty conscience. Cautiously he said, "My eyes aren't twenty-twenty."

"This is not a *trick* question," she fired back.

*Trick* echoed. He'd found the glasses on the dashboard, and she must've looked through the lenses and seen the ear piece. He thought fast. "The doc says my problem is astigmatism aggravated by eye fatigue." *At least the eye fatigue is true.*

"Ha! You said your eyes weren't twenty-twenty."

"Actually they're better than that. One person in a million is blessed with vision that supersedes the normal." *All my eye exams had borne that out.*

"Superman in Clark Kent glasses. Is that it?"

Clay shifted in the seat. Perspiration formed on his upper lip. *Oh, the web you weave . . .*

The air bristled. Terri huffed. In his mind he listed the remaining stops, Albuquerque, Amarillo, Dallas, and on to Fiddle. Surely he could hold out that long. Texans always honor their oaths. It'd been drilled into him. Besides in his heart he believed it was best . . . for the time being.

Terri was uneasy. At least the Luck had worked up to par. Harvick's farewell "good luck" rang in her ears. *The whole world knows now.* Pressure building she had to admit Clay had a working knowledge of horses. Alfred said he'd do fine and he was right. It was herself she worried about. How could she have feelings for someone who is . . . is . . . evasive? Why is he like that? What about the Hally Trick glasses? Is he on the level? One thing for sure, no more nonsense like last night. His question intruded her musings.

"How was the shower? Did you remember the foot powder?"

*No way am I going to tell him what happened.* "Yes. I remembered the foot powder."

"I heard you scrambling around."

"Kind of tight quarters. I tripped."

Turning from him she executed as much body language as she could muster. Not only had she tripped, but dropped her bra in the commode as well. Frustrated she'd rinsed the bra, wrapped it in a paper towel, and stuffed it in her hip pocket. The dampness was coming through too. Stretching the seatbelt as far as it would go, she lifted her hips and pulled down her sweatshirt.

Coming up on the New Mexico state line, Clay stopped for breakfast at a much healthier restaurant. After last night's candy bars Terri ordered fiber-plus cereal, orange juice, and decaf coffee. She expected a comment from Clay, but he was as preoccupied as she was. In the restroom she wrapped a fresh paper towel around the damp bra and stuffed it back in her pocket.

On an on they traveled. She couldn't help but notice his ear-to-ear grin. Ear! The ear piece. Maybe the glasses are from one of those discount stores she reasoned. Maybe that's all he could afford. In any case she'd call Rudd tonight. Surely information about Clay Moore would be zinging the grapevine gossip line.

"Terri."

His voice was too serious. She braced herself. "Yes?"

"When this showdown is over we're going to have a long conversation. I'd like to have it now, but I can't. Ever make a promise to someone, and then wish you could break it?"

"Promises are special. The truth is special too. I don't take either one lightly."

He held her with his eyes as long as he dared and drive too. Even behind the orange disks she felt the communication of pleading. *That eyebrow pencil is special to him. I know it is. Probably has a significant other. He did say he wasn't married. He also said he left the briefcase with Rudd.*

Miles passed before he asked, "What are you thinking?"

"About the puissance wall," she said, her voice calculating. "Actually two puissance walls."

"What's that supposed to mean?"

"After the showdown I'll tell you"—a shadow of smugness crossed her face—"when we have that conversation."

Cutting him off, she concentrated on the scenery. The Western landscape reminded her of the John

Wayne movies Bette had liked. If masked bandits appeared round the bend she wouldn't have been surprised.

"Come on, Terri. Let's try to stay on the same page."

"All right then. I am thinking of masked bandits."

"How so?" His voice cracked.

"Bette used to watch old Western movies. They could've filmed them here. I mean look at all the places the bad guys could ambush us."

Clay chuckled. "Grandma Bette. What about Grandpa?"

"He was killed in a roping accident years ago. I never knew him. Bette said his hand got caught in the lariat, the horse spooked and dragged him two miles."

His voice softened. "Where's Bette now?"

"She passed away in a nursing home while I was in Ireland. It was all . . . all taken care of by the time I got back. Martin Riggs had a hand in it."

"I'm sorry, Terri. That's a tough one."

The concern in his voice was hard to deny. Daryl had wanted her to find out if the nursing home had kept any of Bette's money. The house, he'd said, was worth something. She'd tried to explain the sale of the house had paid for her care.

When Clay exited onto a rest area, she inched forward. The orange-pink adobe huts with their cut-out windows were charming. Under a scrubby tree an Indian woman sat cross-legged in front of a colorful blanket. Sprinkled on the handwoven square was an assortment of silver and turquoise jewelry catching sunlight.

As soon as Clay braked she was out the truck and on the trailer fender. Unlatching the window beside Greenie's head, she said, "Let's take him out and walk him around."

Without spoken communication they backed the horse down the ramp. Clay caught the lead line dangling from the halter. Terri perched on a large rock near the trailer. With the eye of the toughest judge alive, she observed every move of the horse and handler. Satisfied no signs of colic appeared and Clay had the situation in hand, she relaxed. While the sun warmed her face, the damp wad in her pocket pressed against her hip.

With Greenie back in the trailer, she headed for the restroom. Thankful for the heat element attached to the wall she removed the soaked paper towel from her pocket, tossed it, and held the bra under the blast of hot air. When the element cut off she hit the on button again and again. Satisfied the garment was dry, she bent over and held her hip next to the nozzle. When her jeans felt dry she debated putting on the bra, but the drying procedure had taken so long. Not particularly endowed, she figured she was decent and stuffed the bra in her back pocket.

After meticulous checking of the trailer hitch, Clay climbed in the truck where she waited for him. His expert driving was beyond giving her pause for thought.

"Radio?" she asked, hand on the knob.

Clay sighed. "You don't have to ask."

Song after song, mile after mile, Terri focused on her riding experience in Ireland. The fences—all constructed of natural elements ranging from timber to rock—she and Greenie had executed were challenging. Proud of Greenie for never having balked at any obstacle, she wondered if it was enough, enough to beat Roy Scott and the Swan.

Then there was the business of Clay Moore. She didn't want to go there, but she couldn't help it. What would happen to him after this was over? No more singing, no more stirring up emotions best left alone. What about the briefcase? The eyebrow pencil? I don't understand.

When the station focused on country music hits he couldn't resist. "What's your favorite Brooks and Dunn?"

"My Maria," she replied.

Clay chuckled. "Mine too. That's a good sign."

"Sign for what?"

"The more we agree, the more"—he thrust back his shoulders and boomed—"team power."

"Ever thought of career in drama?"

"Actually"—he paused as if considering it—"no."

He gave her such an appealing smile she drew in, checked the gray upholstery separating them, and added another row to her private puissance wall. On second thought she piled on additional rows until they passed the sexy way his luscious dark hair curled at his shirt collar.

Their stops were brief and to the point. Gas and food. Ever conscious of what was at stake, she read labels for sugar and carbohydrate levels and was shocked. The sugar content in a package of dried bananas, pineapples, nuts, and raisins was outrageous, but it seemed more nutritious. She bought a six-pack of bottled spring water.

By the time they pulled in the Albuquerque horse motel, three days on the road had begun to take its toll. While Clay searched for the proprietor she leaned against the hot, dusty truck. A roadrunner appeared at the edge of the lane. She blinked and it was gone. Clay's voice startled her.

"The owner is a little on the skeptical side. I had to pay upfront," he said, his voice weary.

Probably been burned over collecting payments. It'd happened at Bennington's. "What stall do we have?"

"Madame Battle-ax said to take our pick. There's three empties in the middle of the aisle."

The outstanding cleanliness of the stables reminded Terri of Bennington's. A flashback of sweeping the dirt aisle and knocking down cobwebs from every nook and cranny had made her forever grateful for Alfred's rescue. Rider Only was in her contract. Still it was an older wooden structure. Scalloped edges gnawed by a host of bored horses gave her pause.

"I'm checking the stall one more time," she said. "All we need is a splinter to stab Greenie and gangrene to set in."

Clucking to the horse she tapped his hip until he moved over to give her room. Up on her toes she ran her hands over the walls searching for a protruding nail or a snagged board. When she bent over to check the bottom half of the stall, Greenie began nibbling the back of her shirt.

"Quit that," she reprimanded elbowing him off.

Absorbed in her inspections she was aware of Greenie's closeness, but not of his lips fondling her hip pocket.

Clay's laughter rang up to the rafters.

She looked up. Her eyes bulged. Green Luck had her bra clamped between its teeth. Not satisfied to keep the prize inside the stall, he thrust his elegant gray head out the top half of the stall door for all the world to see.

Poking the horse in the chest she repeated "back, back, back" until the horse complied and withdrew his head. Aware of Clay's scrutiny, she reached up to grab the bra, but Greenie had other ideas. Play time! With each attempt to snatch it away, the horse tossed his head higher. The strap hooked on his ear causing major head shaking.

Clay eased inside. Respectful of his height and with as much dignity as she could muster, she stepped aside. Softly placing his hand on Greenie's neck, he began to croon "easy, easy, easy." She watched his touch, heard his voice produce magic. Slowly the Luck lowered his head until his purple-brown eyes were level with Clay's belt buckle. He simply plucked the bra from Greenie's relaxed condition.

"Team power at work," he said handing her the garment.

Stuffing it in her hip pocket she managed, "Thank you."

He pinned her with his eyes. "I know one thing."

"What's that?" His close proximity was getting to her.

"Together we can handle everything. Together is best."

Something in his voice sent a message. A message that put her on defense. "There's a line, buddy. Don't cross it. Underwear removal is not an option."

Clay sighed and ran his hand over the horse's back. "Greenie"—he sighed again—"did you hear that? Terri says we can't be bra snatchers."

She had to bite her tongue. Leaving him in the stall she went about the business of getting the horse settled for the night. Silently he took the water bucket from her hand and, with his usual lack of wasted motion, finished the job.

Somebody somewhere had to have heard of Clay Moore, she thought. Surely the showdown has generated all kinds of speculation. No stone would have been left unturned by the ever-curious horse people.

She knew. She was one of them. Anxious for privacy and a phone call to Rudd was a must.

The motel turned out to be a double-decker with Clay on the second floor, Terri on the first. A dining room off from the lobby looked like a good deal. The quicker they ate, the quicker they'd get a good night's sleep. The uneven rest of the night in the pickup had caught up. Besides, she told Clay, she needed to make a phone call. She hoped he'd assume it was someone special.

Clay confessed to paperwork. He wanted to tally the expenditures for a full accounting to Alfred. Terri dug in her bag for the few receipts she'd saved and offered them to him. He took her hand and held it longer than necessary.

"I'm going to miss my sleeping partner," he whispered, his voice husky.

Her senses leaping to life strained her voice. "Goodnight, Clay."

Slipping inside the motel room, she shut the door behind her and counted to ten. The room was clean, the bed inviting, but the privacy of a phone call to Rudd took precedence. Time zone change in mind, she showered and washed her hair. Positive he'd finished the afternoon work outs, she perched on the edge of the bed, cell phone in hand.

After fourteen disappointing rings, she tried the main office. Twelve rings. As last resort she dialed the all-purpose wall phone beside the wash stall. Half the time it was out of order, or busy. On the first ring she was shocked by an out of breath, "Yo!"

"Rick?"

"Yeah. Is this Terri?" Before she could reply, he groaned, "Hang on a minute. I've got an orangutan in the aisleway."

She could hear him clucking to the horse followed by the squeaky pull of the stall door. She felt a twinge of homesickness. When he came back on the line, she said, "Must be Courier up to old tricks."

Rick laughed. "You got it. What's up?"

"Is Rudd around? I need to talk to him."

"You mean you haven't heard?" he exclaimed.

Alarmed she asked, "Heard what?"

"Maggie had to drag him to the hospital last night. They say he was bucking and rearing, but she got him there."

Her heart sank. "Why? Is he okay?"

"Some kind of ulcer attack. He's scheduled for tests today. Alfred's been at the hospital all night."

"I need to be there," she declared.

"You need to win." Rick sighed. "The scuttlebutt is Rudd's gotten himself worked up over this show-down. He thinks his entire career is on the line. Maggie's being a brick. I don't know what he'd do without her."

"Please tell him not to worry. Tell him we'll win."

"I don't know if I can. He's in ICU," Rick lamented.

"ICU!" Terri choked. "What are the doctors saying?"

"All I know is the head honcho told Maggie his diet had to change, and he had to manage stress better."

"Is he going to be all right?"

Before answering Rick responded to the racket going on in the aisle way. "I've got him," he hollered. "Look, Terri, I've got to go. You know how it is."

"Bye" stuck in her throat. A wave of nausea swept over her.

## Chapter Nine

Standing in front of the TV, Robert Bromwell flicked the remote. Settling on the news channel he lounged across the bed and pulled the duffel bag next to him. Tugging the briefcase from the depths, he smiled as he opened it. Underneath a copy of *Ten Tips To Conquer Colic,* two horse charts, a layman's OR hydraulic lift sketch, and a detailed account of Clay Moore Equine Transportation expenditures he found the scientific-diet research papers. He needed to note his conclusion.

First he called Alfred, left an all's-well message with Henry, his housekeeper. Madame Battle-ax informed him that if she had to call there'd be an extra charge. Clay assured her that'd be no problem. The problem would be if there was one and she didn't call.

Next he checked in with Tony at the clinic. Updates were given, crises evaluated, anedotes shared, and the local weather reported. Soon he began experiencing a fleeting alarm of losing control of his clinic, his baby. Even Old Man Coleman had conceded to let Tony give his stallion the West Nile Virus shot. All the while, Terri's research folder rested on his knees.

Bracing a pillow against the headboard, he leaned back and opened the folder. In the garage apartment bathroom the medicine cabinet door, hanging by one hinge, had exposed her vitamins. It was a start. For research purposes he'd listed them. Glancing over the articles clipped from various medical journals and nutrition Bibles for athletes, he read his comments scribbled in the margins.

She's on the right path. Candy bar consumption is definitely down, but does that make a difference in the stamina to go the course? Is hyperactivity a factor? Probably, but how much he didn't know. It wasn't his top priority. Terri was. On the last page he penned his final notation.

He wanted to sing. He wanted Terri cuddled in his arms. He wanted to share the problems he was having with the hydraulic lift in the clinic's OR. He wanted her to meet his cat, Mecate. Heck, he just wanted her.

It'd had been a long night of sleepless tossing and turning. Now waiting for Clay, she stared at the packed luggage clustered at her feet. She picked at the sleeve of her purple sweatshirt. Her complexion was not on her mind. At the first tap at the door, she was there.

In two short strides, Clay crossed the space separating them. Gently taking her by the shoulders, he looked deeply into her eyes. Brows wrinkled, voice soft and caring, he asked, "What's the matter?"

"Rudd's in the hospital."

Clay leaned closer. "What happened?"

"He . . . he had an ulcer attack. Rick says he's in ICU."

He took her in his arms. Burying his lips next to her ear, he whispered, "He'll be all right."

Yielding to the comfort of his arms, she rested her face against his chest. "Rick says to call back for a report around noon. They're doing tests this morning."

Massaging the small of her back, he brought her closer to him.

"Rick said"—she sniffed against his shirt—"Rudd thinks his career is on the line over this showdown. The doc told Maggie he had to watch his diet and manage stress."

Her spoken fears had a disarming effect. She began disengaging herself from his grasp. "Come on," she said her voice uneven. "Let's get this show on the road."

Taking advantage of the breakfast bar located off the lobby, they joined several zombielike travelers already in line. Shuffling past trays and bumping her

head on the plastic dome overtop, she chose can-
taloupe slices, a bagel, and decaf coffee. Seated in an
avocado-and-orange booth, Clay reminded her of
Rudd's excellent physical condition, the marvels of
modern medicine, and gave her a detailed accounting of an endoscopy exam.

Looking at him in despair, she croaked, "But the
intensive care unit, Clay. That's serious."

"It's the best place," he assured her. "They'll monitor his stats and be on hand for the slightest change."

Terri sucked in. Through narrow lips, she stated,
"No more nonsense, Clay. We *have* to be team."

"I'll speak to Green Luck."

"What do you mean?" she asked puzzled.

He gave her his most engaging grin. "We can't
have him undressing you, can we?"

She felt warm inside. *He's trying to get me to lighten
up.* "Alfred always said he was a talented horse."

At the Albuquerque horse motel, a senior citizen
greeted them. With all the moves of a seasoned horseman he went about the business of checking Greenie's
stablemates, a gelding and two mares. Thoughtfully
he said he'd wait until they were finished before he
fed.

As soon as Clay tacked Green Luck Terri mounted
and, with the senior citizen's permission, entered the
ring next to the stables. Letters of the alphabet lining
the fence signaled dressage horses worked here. Tak-

ing a deep breath, she collected herself and concentrated on cueing Greenie. The workout went quickly.

Supplies packed, Greenie loaded, Clay took the tourist's route through the old town of Albuquerque. No comment was made as they passed an inviting candy store on a street corner.

Turning on to Route 40 headed for Amarillo, he asked, "What's your take on Alfred?"

"He's a wing-dingy!" she declared off the top of her head. Thoughtfully her tone changed. "Lately so much of the worry has fallen on Rudd. No wonder he's got an ulcer."

"Uh, Terri."

"Uh, Clay," she mimicked.

"Alfred's one of the best friends I've ever had. He showed faith in me when a lot of people did not. I'll do anything for him. Anything," he repeated.

His petitioning voice was a little disturbing. Maybe he was a wild and rebellious youth. Maybe Alfred had rescued him and became his mentor. "That means," she said, "getting us to Fiddle and being one heck of an attendant."

"Just remember Alfred's so hung up on psyching out Cora, Roy Scott, Roger Hill, and even the Swan, that he's gone to unusual extremes."

Terri agreed. "You'll never believe what he had me do."

Clay glanced at her. "What was that?"

"About a month ago Cora's granddaughter, Kristin, was in California looking at horses. She stopped by to see Alfred. Don't you know he made me hide Greenie in the garage until she left? I couldn't believe it! I thought he was losing it. Now, I see his motivation."

"Alfred likes to keep his cards close to his vest."

She agreed with a bob of her chin.

Checking mileage and the time, they were, according to Clay, making excellent progress. When he stopped for gas she waited for him to unlatch Greenie's door and watched as the horse thrust his head through the opening. While he was busy at the pump, she ducked behind the back of the trailer. Rick answered on the sixth ring.

"Terri, here. What's the news on Rudd?"

"Martin Riggs and Alfred just left. They said Rudd rested comfortably last night. They're waiting on lab report results. If everything's okay he's going to be moved to a private room. After a procedure he might be discharged."

"That sounds good. How's Maggie holding up?"

Rick laughed. "Riggs said she'd got everybody marching to her drum. You know how she is when it comes to Rudd. She's already signed up for a nutrition class."

Peeking around the corner of the trailer she checked the whereabouts of Clay. She tried to sound normal. "Heard anything about Clay Moore?"

"Alfred says he's a good hand. That's it."

"No gossip?" she asked hopefully.

A tractor trailer pulled in snorting and wheezing brakes. She didn't hear Rick's reply, only a dead dial tone.

One look at his passenger and Clay softened his humming. Gradually he tapered off and stopped. Granted Alfred had gambled letting him try his procedure on his grand prix horse. The benefits reaped from the success had amazed him, but this imposter charade bordered on the ridiculous. There's no reason Terri can't be in on it. He'd have a talk with Alfred tonight.

Terri stretched as much as she could with the seatbelt restraining her rib cage. Yawning, she looked over at Clay.

"I thought you'd never wake up. Want to smell something?" Not waiting for a reply he hit the electric window buttons. A gust of warm air filled the cab.

Drowsy, she gave him a funny look. "Are you crazy?"

He filled his lungs and grinned at her. "Try it."

Terri sucked in. "Jeez! I don't believe it."

Closing the windows, he laughed. "Ah," he expounded his voice melodramatic, "the scent left behind by a thousand cattle herds. Think of the history, *Texas* history."

Terri pinched her nose.

Undeterred he announced, "Amarillo coming up."

She had to smile. "Glad to be in your home state?"

"Yes, Terri, I am."

The sincerity expressed tugged at her heart. Checking out the brown flat terrain dotted with windmills beside water tanks, she imagined a home, a real home.

Exiting off Route 40 in search of the horse motel Clay hit a bump. The trailer lurched. Terri snapped to attention. The Caballo Motel sign tacked to a stunted mesquite at the head of a lane displayed a red arrow. Turning in they passed a mission bell on a post. Coming round the corner of the stables was the tallest, leanest Texan Terri had ever seen.

"Think we should offer to feed him?" Clay quipped.

Terri giggled.

The Texan introduced himself as Dusty Moraes. In the same breath he declared he wasn't kin to Adriano. Terri gave him a blank look. Clay explained Adriano Moraes was a top bull rider. Offering his hand to Clay, Dusty told them he'd been expecting them. When he said newspaper reporters were at the house, both Clay and Terri looked snakebit.

"Hope you don't mind giving an interview," Dusty said.

"No, not at all," Clay replied, his voice reserved.

Terri came to the point. "How did they know about us?"

Dusty scratched his chin. "Heck, lady, it's been on the horse channel and in the papers, a match between two old adversaries. When I was down at the feed store and told them about your reservations, they wanted an interview."

Stalling to consider this development, Terri and Clay ambled over to the stables. Constructed of mix-matched materials ranging from cinder blocks to plywood, Terri was amazed at the ingenuity the way the materials were used. One stall front was fashioned out of welded hubcaps. Friendly heads, quarter horse breeding, poked out and nickered to the strangers. A tin cup hung on a nail above a water pump just inside the door.

Dusty, a smile of pride on his face, followed behind and pointed out the stall he'd readied for them. When they unloaded Green Luck he was there to lend a hand.

"That's a tall drink of water you got there," he drawled, backing off to observe Greenie's conformation.

Clay chuckled. He was about to reply when two ladies dressed in T-shirts and jeans approached. The short one with a single gray plait down to her waist carried a tape recorder. Toting a digital camera her partner was almost as tall and thin as Dusty. The pair introduced themselves as reporters for the feed store's monthly newsletter.

Terri breathed easier. At least the article wouldn't be seen by Alfred. She dreaded his reaction if the tiniest bit of information regarding Green Luck or herself got out. She made eye contact with Clay. Partially hidden by Green Luck's massive shoulder he wiped imaginary sweat from his brow. Knowing they were on the same page was a relief.

Yes, she told the reporters, Cora Stuart and Alfred McDonnell were going head to head at Jake Bob Johnson's arena in Fiddle. No, she'd never competed against Roy Scott and Bewick Swan. The puissance wall caught them off guard. She explained it was a wall made of hollow wooden blocks. Rows were added until a horse failed to clear it.

Thoughtfully Clay handed Terri her velvet hunt cap for pictures. Definitely aware of the fuss being made over him, Green Luck stood four square. Pricking his ears forward and remaining stock-still he seemed to swell in size before their very eyes.

When the stall door was pulled shut for the last time, Terri and Clay thanked Dusty for his help with hosing down the trailer mat and hauling supplies to the stall. As they were leaving, Terri was jostled by a small boy generating a cloud of dust.

"Whoa, son," Dusty said. "Watch where you're going."

"Mamma said to tell you the barbecue was ready."

"Mmmmmmmm, doggies." Dusty licked his lips.

"Mamma said to bring these people. We got plenty."

Dusty looked to Clay and Terri. "Me and Justin, here, don't want to upset Mamasita. Please join us."

Texas barbeque smells wafted under their noses. Faint laughter filled the background. All thoughts of fruits and vegetables vanished. Simultaneously they accepted.

The barbeque was set up in the yard behind the white-and-green shuttered mobile home. It didn't take long for Terri to verify the tall, thin reporter was Dusty's sister. Her husband, an inch shorter, had the shoulders and arms of a professional bull rider.

Mamasita turned out to be a petite Mexican ball of fire. *Sí,* she told Terri, my name is Maria. Welcome to our home. Hustling round the table made from a discarded door, braced by cinder block legs, Maria checked on the food fit for kings. Terri helped bring out the paper plates, cups, and plastic utensils from the kitchen. Next to the table, a grill loaded with ribs sizzled and smoked. Dusty yelled gangway when he brought out a cast iron pot of steaming chili.

At the table sandwiched between Clay and Justin, Terri listened to the child's and Clay's back and forth commentary on the Dallas Cowboys and was amazed at the infinite details they knew. Maria corrected Justin several times for pestering the guest, but he wasn't alone. Everyone at the table seemed to have an opinion on the quarterback.

Terri ate until she was full and then filled her plate again simply because it tasted so good. If she'd known about the chocolate cake, she would have saved room. Instead she made room.

All the while Dusty and his sister teased each other outrageously. When Maria felt it'd gone far enough she put her foot down. Immediately the bantering quieted. Nobody messes with the cook, seemed to be the general consensus. Compliments gushed and disguised belches ensued.

Justin wiggled backward off the bench and got his football from behind the tree. Clay jumped up, jarring the table. Justin tossed the ball to him. Fading back, the ball at his shoulder, Clay faked a pass before he threw it. Justin missed. The ball bounced against the grill.

Maria jumped up. "That's enough," she ordered.

Justin obeyed grumbling.

"Aw, mom," Clay teased and sat back down.

This is a real family Terri mused making room for Clay.

Texas stars came out. Lanterns were lit. The party was just beginning and they had to find a motel for the night. Terri offered to help with the clean-up, but Maria wouldn't hear of it. Besides Gramps was coming over later. After thanking everyone for the feast, she and Clay began the trek back to the stables and a final check on Greenie.

Slipping his arm around her, Clay said, "Nice family."

Misgivings began to fade. Nodding she smiled at him.

Clay topped off Green Luck's water bucket. Slowly pulling the stall door shut he brushed against Terri. He was so close. The dark, shadowy stables, the contentment of a fine evening relaxed her defenses. Her whole being seemed to be filled with anticipation. When he took her in his arms, her soft curves molded to his lean body.

Closing her eyes, she tilted her chin. Just when she expected his lips to touch hers the pencil clipped to the small pad in his shirt pocket stabbed her shoulder. The wake-up call stiffened her body.

"What's wrong?" Huskiness lingered in his tone.

Scarcely aware of her own voice, she blurted, "Why don't you kiss the owner of the eyebrow pencil?"

He moved one step backward. "Is that what's bothering you? I can explain."

*This is your last chance.* She held her breath.

"It belongs to my mother."

The absurdity of his answer flew all over her. "Yeah. Right. And she gave it to you on her death bed."

One look at his eyes, and she knew she'd gone too far. Refusing to back down, she glared at him. The old haunting pain of being used swept through her. What happened next baffled her.

"Let me show you something," he said, his jaws tight. Alfred be damned. He grabbed a rag off a peg, clasped his free hand around her wrist, and steered her to the water pump. Shoving his glasses to the top of his head, he revealed a pair of very stormy gray eyes. She drew in at the sight.

He pumped just once. It was enough to dampen the rag. Holding it close to his face, he said, "Give me a minute."

She was about to ask if he had something in his eye when a thunderbolt of commotion tore around the corner and nearly bumped into them.

"Daddy wants to know if he's to feed for you in the morning?" Justin asked huffing and puffing.

Terri didn't trust her voice. She watched Clay work at transforming his look of intent to one of consideration.

"No," he said to the child. "Tell your dad we'll feed after Terri works the horse. Thanks for asking."

Justin's voice full on energy sang out, "Okay."

He took off in the same manner he'd arrived. Terri marched out behind him, leaving Clay with a damp rag hovering near his eyebrows, a fist on his hip.

She slammed the pickup door. Clay jumped in, slid under the wheel, and jammed the key into the ignition. Barreling out the lane, he headed toward the town of Amarillo. At the first motel he came to he pulled in. Of all the motels in the Lone Star state of Texas this was the rattiest.

## Chapter Ten

One glance at the garish neon VACANCY sign, the seedy office entrance, the trash littering the parking spaces and Clay knew it was a mistake, but he'd made his decision and he was sticking to it. He needed privacy and a phone.

Hand on a scummy knob, he opened the door for Terri. In record speed he'd unloaded the truck with her things and departed. Purposefully he kept the orange disks covering the fake lens of the Hally Tricks frames. Somehow it helped to have a barrier between her eyes and his. He didn't need to be reminded of the honesty shining in hers, the dishonesty lurking in his. That Justin had interrupted him from washing off the eye make-up was a wake-up call. He'd had enough.

He tried Alfred's stable office phone. Whistling

through clenched teeth he counted ten rings. Next he tried his home number. Pacing back and forth he attempted telepathy to get to Alfred.

He could hear Terri now. Real men don't wear eyebrow makeup. She'd no more believed the pencil belonged to his mother than he would have in her boots. The irony was it'd been the only truthful revelation he'd made concerning his appearance. The pencil *did* belong to his mother. She'd left it behind on her last visit. If she hadn't he would've had to buy one. Then, gritting his teeth, he could have told her he'd bought it for himself. He cringed at the kind of response that would've brought.

Regret in his heart he felt like kicking himself. Alfred needed him because of Greenie's history of colic and at the same time he wanted everything kept secret. Why he mentioned a disguise was beyond him. He'd sworn a Texas-sized oath not to reveal his identity. He didn't swear he wouldn't fall for his rider. During his youth and beyond he'd experienced chemistry, but never had the dimension of caring, cherishing, loving been a part.

He tried again. The irritating buzz-buzz-buzz caused him to shake the phone. In his mind he went back to the night Alfred agreed to let him perform the surgery. His horse was a prime candidate. Having faith the procedure would prevent a fatality, he could still see the concern, the trust in Alfred's eyes. If he'd confessed to

Terri before checking with him first those hazel orbs would haunt him the rest of his life. He knew it. Painful as it was going back on his word was not in his character.

He pushed the redial button. Alfred answered on the second ring. "I just finished talking to Terri," he said, his voice normal. "She says you're doing a great job, but she's worried about—how did she put it?— your background. She wanted to know how long I'd known you."

"Any chance of me telling her?" he asked, easing into the subject gently.

"No, indeed," Alfred blustered. "I'll take full responsibility for any problems your identity creates. I have a plan for that."

His heart sank. He knew from his tone he wouldn't relent. "Care to share that plan?"

Alfred grunted.

A chink and a roll like the throw of dice hit a surface near the phone. Without the hearing aid, talking to Alfred was fruitless. Shouting goodnight as loud as he dared, he hung up. Seldom did he curse, but before the night was over he'd outdone himself.

Terri waited in the motel room bags in hand. When footsteps stopped at the door she swung it open and caught Clay with knuckles in the air.

"Got everything?" she snapped.

"My stuff is already in the truck."

"What about your mother's eyebrow pencil?" she taunted.

"That too." He winced.

On the ride to the Caballo Motel, Terri bristled. The air between them snapped and crackled.

"About the pencil—" Clay started.

"Forget the pencil!"

"No, I don't want to. My mother left it behind on her last visit. That is the gospel truth."

Did he expect her to believe that? USE TERRI, SHE'S HANDY, must be stenciled in red on her forehead. Daryl had read it and now Clay. Somehow she'd thought Clay was different. He'd made her feel special, but how she could trust him when he acted like two people?

As he pulled out in traffic she automatically glanced over her shoulder to check the trailer's position through the rear window. What she saw on the bench seat was yet another ugly reminder. Nestled in the corner Clay's duffel bag had four protruding points in the shape of a briefcase.

Not another word was spoken. As they approached the Caballo Motel lane the red-orange Texas sun appeared on the horizon. Silver and pink streaked the gray skies.

Dusty joined them at the stalls. While Clay saddled Green Luck he asked questions about English tack. Terri waited in silence. Bracing herself for a leg up she mounted awkwardly. Atop the horse she could see the crown of Dusty's ball cap and Clay's bare head.

"Anything I should know about the field?" she asked, pointing to the back of the stables. Three red-and-white striped barrels were set up in a racing position.

"The smoothest path is around the barrels," Dusty said, his eyes twinkling.

Terri smiled at him. "Greenie would rather jump them."

At the edge of the field she broke into an easy trot, welcoming the breeze brushing across her face. Concentrating on her work out she began to imagine she was in Jake Bob's arena—lights, crowd, Alfred on the rail, Cora nearby. One false move and it'd all be over. Rudd's advice, never allow distractions, rang in her ears.

Taking Green Luck at a walk she had a panic moment. Maybe Alfred should've gone with Courier, a proven horse, one with a record. So many things could go wrong. Cora could be as crafty as Alfred. "No distractions, no distractions" echoed in her head like a mantra. Leaning forward in the saddle she picked up the pace and set her mind on winning.

She could feel Greenie working well, paying attention to her cues, and if the barrels magically turned into a six-foot wall, she knew they'd clear it. Smiling she reined the horse beside Clay and Dusty. Both men looked up at her.

As she leaned over the saddle to ask Clay what he thought of Greenie's smooth canter, a stiff breeze lifted a lock of luscious raven hair from his forehead. She blinked. Her eyes bulged. Draping the upper part of her body over Greenie's neck, on the pretense of adjusting the bridle, she side-glanced the top of Clay's head. The swirl made by an accommodating wind gust revealed exactly what she'd suspected. His roots were sandy.

Clay Moore had dyed his hair! Why? screamed through her brain. It couldn't be vanity or he wouldn't wear those funky glasses. Funky fake glasses! It hit her with a thud. This man is an impostor. Shaken by the revelation, she found it impossible to comprehend the conversation aimed up at her.

When she and Dusty stood side by side watching Clay walk down the horse, his remarks went in one ear and out the other. Normally she'd have responded cheerfully, but this was not normal. Chalky-faced, she clasped and unclasped her hands.

Running across the field, book bag pounding on his small shoulders, Justin diverted her anxiety. "Terri! Terri! Mama says that's the tallest horse she's ever seen."

"You better head on out to the end of the lane, son," Dusty said. "You're going to miss the school bus."

"Yuck. Double yuck." Justin pouted.

"Triple yuck if you miss it. Vamos!" Dusty warned.

Kicking dirt clumps on purpose, Justin started

off, but not before he turned and waved at Terri and Clay.

Greenie loaded, hay bag checked, grain poured out on the shelf under its nose, Clay approached Dusty with his hand over the wallet in his hip pocket. At the very last minute Maria showed up with plastic cups of coffee for them. After good-byes and good lucks, they climbed in the cab and started down the lane. The trailer hit a rut. Greenie neighed.

"Take it easy," Terri griped. "You're upsetting Greenie and sloshing my coffee."

Easing the rig to a complete stop Clay removed his glasses and draped his arm across the back of the seat. "Terri," he said gently, "about the pencil . . ."

On and on he went about how he could explain everything when the Super Bowl was over, but for the moment she had to trust him. Terri heard his voice droning over her panicked thoughts. *This man is an impostor. How can that be? I don't understand. What is Alfred going to say? What should I do?* Slowly she became aware the cab was deathly quiet.

"What?" she asked mildly confused. "What did you say?"

Clay huffed and revved the motor. On Route 40 headed for Dallas they rumbled through plains, small towns, fair-sized cities, and back to plains. Stopping only for food and fuel, they became too businesslike, too polite.

"Yes, ma'am, I checked the trailer hitch."

"Thank you."

"Care to share a candy bar?"

"May I respectfully point out your nerves appear to be jittery?"

"Leave my nerves out of this."

"Yes, ma'am."

She fidgeted with the strap of her canvas bag. He's a fraud! A fraud who'd lied about the briefcase, lied about the glasses. Even his hair is a lie! He'd said he owed Alfred. That's probably a lie too. No way could she discuss this with Rudd, not in his condition. Stress on top of an ulcer is not a good thing.

She returned to square one. If he isn't Clay Moore, then who is he? Did Cora have something to do with this? After all this is the final showdown. All stops are pulled. Her facial muscles pinched. If this man does one thing to upset Alfred she wouldn't be responsible for her actions. That much she knew.

The more she thought about it, the more she wondered if the answer laid at Cora's feet. Had she gotten a spy in the camp? Someone who would help her turn tables on Alfred at the final blowout. She could hear Cora saying to Alfred, oh, yes, the seventeen hands gray Irish thoroughbred, draft cross. The rider eats candy bars and has a tendency to let her enthusiasm outweigh her determination to win.

She let that thought fester. Cora must have had a hand in shuffling the drivers, she deduced. *I don't see how she did it, but she must have.* After all when Greenie had colic it was Robert that Alfred wanted to talk to, not Clay Moore.

"Does Alfred know Robert, your partner?" she asked, trying to suppress the angst in her voice.

"Yes," he replied. "I believe he does."

Of course Alfred knows Robert. He's the one he wanted to hire in the first place. Her feelings, jagged and painful, surfaced. Tears trembled her eyelids. When her heart quieted, it was assaulted once again. If he isn't Clay Moore, then who is he? Was part of the plan to distract the rider? The horror of that thought raised the hair on the back of her neck. Cora might be crafty, but she wasn't criminal. Or was she?

Tense, her stomach cramped, her head ached. Aware of each concerned glance of Clay's didn't help. When they stopped for lunch she excused herself and headed for the restroom. Fingers trembling she fumbled with the cell phone as she dialed Alfred's office number. When Rudd answered she was shocked.

"How are you?" she asked, her voice pitched high.

"Good to go." He chuckled.

"Tell the truth," Terri admonished.

"The doc put me on a diet. Looks like horse feed to me. I could stock a pharmacy with the pills I have to take. Maggie's being a bear about it too."

"Good for her!"

"Easy for you to say," he grumbled. "Now, what about Green Luck?" His voice perked up. "Is he be-having himself?"

"He had a belly ache in Flagstaff, not bad. He's working good. This morning was exceptional."

Rudd gave a worried sigh. "How about your assistant?"

"He's on par with you and Alfred when it comes to handling Greenie," she said truthfully. "Is our boss handy?"

"He and Riggs left about an hour ago. Jake Bob's to meet them at the airport."

Hiding her disappointment, she asked brightly, "Heard anything about our competition?"

"Not a cursed thing," he replied agitated. "I think Cora's taking lessons from Alfred."

Misgivings growing by the minute she said her good-byes. Leaving the restroom she had her guard up more than ever. Clay met her halfway. She reported in the tone of a drill sergeant that Rudd had been discharged.

Inside the cab she watched as he deftly turned the pages of the horse travel guide book. Inner torment gnawing, she waited while he checked the directions.

"What's the problem?" she asked, fuming under the surface.

"Looks like the Dallas horse motel is in the middle of a residential section."

"How long will it take to get there?"

Clay paused. "Hour and a half. Two at the max."

He looked at her with such appealing tenderness she had trouble quelling the dull ache of foreboding.

"Good," she said. "The sooner this trip's over, the better."

The Texas sun glared through the windshield. She squinted through her sunglasses. Finally she dug in her canvas bag and pulled up a yellow ball cap, JUST JUMP IT stitched in green across the front. Tucking her leg under her, she scrunched around until her back was totally facing Clay. With troubled eyes she focused on the silver door handle, snug within a cocoon of gray upholstery, and struggled with her worries.

She didn't remember falling asleep. In fact she was shocked by the sight of Clay grinning at her through the window. When he opened the door she unfolded her body and put weight on the leg numbed from her curled sleeping position. Promptly she fell into his arms.

Laughter floated up from his throat. "Whoa, little, gal," he Texas drawled. "Take it easy."

Numb from toe to kneecap she had two choices, either rely on his strength or fall on her face. Clay wrapped his arms around her. Heady stuff to be able to smell and almost taste him through his shirt. "Back off" trembled in the recesses of her mind while her heart whispered "one second, one more second." His ragged breath wafting across her ear didn't help.

The footsteps in the background and Greenie pawing the trailer mat gave her a jolt. Mind overruling heart, she backed off.

"Who are you?" she practically screamed. "Clay Manure?"

His eyebrows shot up. "What do you mean?"

"Clay Moore?" she questioned, her chin jutted. "More like Clay Manure."

A group of riders and grooms of the horses registered at the horse motel gathered round at a respectable distance. All had their ears trained on the argument taking place. Clay could see them beyond Terri's shoulder. The horse of one of the rider's had been treated at his clinic.

"Hush," he said, making a face, raising a brow. "There's a crowd behind you. We'll talk about this in private."

The brow did it. "Look, Mister Evasive, I don't care! I've had it with your tap dancing around questions."

Taking her by the hand he steered her to the back of the trailer. "Don't talk so loud. You're drawing a crowd."

She jerked free from his hold. Voice full of venom she began spitting out words between clenched teeth. "You lied about the briefcase. I saw you taking it from the truck, and then you boldfaced *lied* about it."

His eyes widened.

Inching forward, the equestrian crowd found amazing busy work to do. One leaned over and examined her boot, another glanced at the sky as if the clouds were a matter of life or death. Another began picking at a clump of weeds looking for who knows what.

"Guess what? You don't have to explain the eyebrow pencil," she growled. "After all, people who dye—"

Clay glared at her. "Don't say another word until we get someplace private. We have Alfred to think of."

"Ha! Alfred! Fat lot you care about him when you're spying for Cora. That's what you've been doing all along."

Clay gave her a look that stopped her cold. Too many ears were hovering. Much as she hated it he made sense. Clamping her jaws tight she went on automatic pilot and performed as a rider would in a horse motel situation.

Somehow they found the proprietor, unloaded Green Luck, and settled him in a stall. The hip-roofed barn had four stalls lining each side of a narrow aisleway. An electric fan hung in every conceivable spot. The whirring prompted Clay to say, "Welcome to Texas weather."

At one time the barn must have been outstanding, but it was obvious that land had been sold off and developed and this lone structure had survived. There was no place left to work Green Luck, Terri observed.

Bits and pieces of conversation of the milling riders indicated they were on their way to a show in the morning. Terri kept to herself. Eventually they ambled out, leaving the facility solely to Clay and Terri. Hands fisted by her side, she started up again.

"I want some answers," she demanded with fire in her eyes.

"Cora knows me," Clay began, toying with her sleeve, "and Alfred wanted to execute a complete surprise to her. I mentioned a disguise—jokingly, I might add—and Alfred took me up on it."

Terri chewed on this. It sounded like Alfred after all the pains he went to keep her and Greenie under wraps. "But if you're not Clay Moore, then who are you?"

"Robert—"

The commotion of the riders returning stopped him cold.

"Yes, yes, go on," Terri encouraged, "Robert what?"

The equestrians froze. One held a foot suspended.

"Brown," he said with a peculiar hitch to his voice. "Robert Daniel Brown."

## Chapter Eleven

The downtown Dallas hotel had all the bells and whistles you could ask for. After agreeing to meet in the lobby by the waterfall in half an hour, Clay escorted Terri to her room and trudged on to his with turmoil in his heart. Ever since Terri believed she'd solved his identity, she'd become so open to him. He wanted to crawl in a hole and die.

Brown, he mused. From his past a Doctor Warren Brown came to mind. He'd had him for anatomy and physiology of reproduction in the mare. Brown, he repeated, digusted with himself. We'll be in Fiddle before noon tomorrow. When Alfred finds out how I feel about Terri he'll understand. The man's not *that* unreasonable.

Terri took a quick shower, slipped on a clean pair

of Wranglers and a yellow knit polo shirt, an English saddle appliqué on the pocket. Joy bubbled in her eyes. Her heart sang with delight. For the first time the shadows clouding round Robert Brown, alias Clay Moore, had dissipated, opening the way for a new perspective on the situation.

If Alfred had told her Clay was Robert, he would've had to tell Rudd. Rudd couldn't have kept it from Maggie, and from there it'd been open season. Man, I bet he's Cora's favorite hauler. Looks like Alfred pulled a fast one.

Thinking of Alfred she warned herself to calm down and get in gear. The ride of her life awaited, but tonight she couldn't contain an anticipation of a different sort. The kind that made her smile and think of the wonderful evening ahead. Even her sprint to the elevator had a spring of eagerness about it.

By the waterfall watching his approach, she was struck by an image of his dark hair as sandy. Blinking away the confusion, she broke into a friendly, open smile as he draped his arm around her shoulder. She knew she glowed.

Both nixed the idea of getting back in the truck. On the street in front of the hotel they looked both ways. Between the mirrored buildings, patches of black Dallas sky twinkled with stars. Hand in hand they ambled toward a place called Texas Hot Chili. Floor littered with peanut shells, a giant TV hanging from the ceiling, and a three-piece combo—guitar, piano, drum—

prompted Robert to take her elbow. Laughing and skipping, they two-stepped to an empty booth.

Raking his arm across the table, he cleared off the peanut shells left by previous occupants. "I like the busted boot cuisine better," he said reaching for her hand.

The sound of clapping to the music exploded in the booth behind her. "What did you say," she asked, her voice strained.

Rising from the bench he leaned over and touched his nose to hers. "I said I miss the busted boot cuisine."

The warm reaction to his flesh brushing hers was becoming all too familiar. Peering deeply into his silver-gray eyes, she managed, "Me too."

A waitress materialized, juggling a tray of hot bowls of spicy chili, salsa, and chips. Patiently she waited for Robert to be seated. He managed a grin and requested mineral water. "You'll need it," she remarked knowingly.

On the way back to the hotel they moseyed along, treasuring every footstep. The feel of his arm around her waist, the way he leaned close to whisper in her ear, created a mood she didn't want disturbed. One she wanted to explore.

By the time they'd arrived at the waterfall, she was as relaxed as she'd been since the trip began. In fact she was downright weak-kneed. When Robert pointed out a gold bug-eyed fish at the base of the fall, she rested her head on his shoulder. In a cloud of happiness she watched the milky-white fins and tail disappear and reappear between the rocks and underwater fern.

Arms entwined they wandered aimlessly to the elevator, rode to the second floor. Inside the cubicle she snuggled close in his arms. They sighed in sync with the swish of the sliding portal, exposing a dimly lit hallway.

At her door he took her in his arms. The kiss, sound and thorough, held promises, leaving her breathless. His last words, "There's more to explain," muffled against her lips were lost in the moment of desire. She did remember placing her palms on his chest and murmuring something, but she couldn't swear to what it was. Inside the hotel room she couldn't swear to anything except she knew she'd never be the same.

The next morning she was up and going before the wake-up call came through. Taking time with her hair, make-up, and clothes, she was keenly aware of a delicious, warming, downright thrilling sensation. Certainly a feeling that'd surpassed anything she'd felt before. She could hardly wait to join Robert Daniel Brown.

A quick breakfast of fruit, oatmeal, and juice at the hotel, and they were on their way to the stables. Proprietor paid, Green Luck loaded, but before they could back out, the riders returned blocking the driveway. Quarters were tight. It was easier to wait than try to maneuver around them.

Terri leaned against the trailer. "Robert, how long will it take to get to Fiddle?"

"Two hours max," he said tracing a finger down her sleeve. "You'd better call me Clay until this is over."

"Good thinking. Who came up with Clay Moore?"

"I did. I'd hoped it'd help Alfred remember my alias, Clayton Moore, the Lone Ranger, the masked do-gooder."

"Hey, that's pretty good!" She gave him an enthusiastic high-five. "Robert Brown will never cross my lips."

He cringed.

Once he'd snaked between the mirrored buildings lining the main fareway through Dallas he picked up speed. He could hardly wait to pigeonhole Alfred and get off the hook. Robert stared straight ahead. He knew if he caught eye contact he'd slam on brakes and cause a wreck. He wanted her in his arms.

"Rudd said rumors are flying at the stables about what's going to happen after this is over."

A camper on his bumper and a rusted-out pickup in front prevented him from pulling over and stopping. He didn't like the sound of her voice. In frustration he tapped the horn. From the side window of the truck a hand appeared, giving him the all American salute. He gripped the steering wheel. Every fiber urged him to pull over.

"I mean we're all pretty tight at the stables. We have our squabbles from time to time, but we always support each other. After this I don't know how Alfred can top himself."

"I don't have a clue, Terri."

"You must have owed Alfred big time to go undercover."

She turned to him for an explanation, an explanation he couldn't give. After a few minutes of strained silence, she said, "Before I put on my game face, I have to tell you."

He glanced in her direction. Chin tucked, she was staring at the floorboard. Silently cursing the timing, he was stymied. The camper behind him was breathing on his rear and the nasty truck in front lagged. If he wasn't careful, he'd miss the exit.

"Please go on," he encouraged. Inching forward, he checked the mirrors and hit the turn signal.

"I'm glad I know the truth about you, the whole truth. I mean I knew you could handle horses, that's a given, but the business with the disguise got to me. You know"—she turned to face him—"half-truths are the worst kind. Believe me. I'm a living example of how cruel that can . . . can be."

Her voice was so soft he held his breath. At the same time he scanned the countryside in search of the brick archway entrance to the Johnson complex.

"My mother died when I was in the third grade." She paused, bitting her lip. "Bette told me she died of heart failure. That was true as far as it went. At school I learned the details. She died of heart failure brought on by pain medication and alcohol. The kids said she was a drunk druggie."

He reached for her hand, brought it to his lips. Almost as quickly he released it to grip the steering wheel.

"I know Bette did it to protect me, but it is the *truth* that protects you and nothing else. I was beginning to think some pretty scary things about you."

Not completely in control of the vehicle he swerved under the elaborate brick arch. Guilt overwhelming him, he had to confess. Mouth open, he turned in time to witness her face change from raw honesty to pure delight and surprise. In a heartbeat the mood had shifted.

"Look!" she exclaimed unfastening the seatbelt. "There's Alfred. Stop! I want out."

Fearing she'd fly from the truck in motion, he braked, holding his breath as she leaped from the cab and ran toward Alfred. Easing the rig behind her, he eventually veered off and pulled in at the designated parking area next to the arena. He watched her wrap her arms around Alfred, toss back her head in laughter. Jake Bob joined in. Give me five minutes with Alfred, he vowed, with or without his blessings this charade is going to stop. I can't hurt her. I can't. I won't.

He hardly knew Jake Bob, but the thought of deceiving him made his stomach queasy. Before joining the group he unlatched the door by Greenie's head. Ears pricked, nostrils flared, the horse gave a long, commanding throat rumble. Whistling through clenched teeth, he approached Jake Bob, Alfred, and Terri.

Jake Bob—a big, burly Texan—wore a straw Stetson, white T-shirt and jeans. His ample stomach overlapped a silver belt buckle the size of a dinner plate. Robert couldn't help but notice his puzzled expression.

Jake Bob scratched his chin. "Dang, you look familiar."

"Clay Moore's the name."

"Haven't we met?" Jake Bob asked.

Terri's expression touched on pure dismay. Alfred began making noises like a rooster with a bad cackle. All attention was drawn to him. Terri patted him on the back and asked over and over if he was okay.

Alfred nodded and pointed toward the lane. Kicking up Texas trail dust the approaching rig displayed the famous silver and navy colors of Stuart Stables. The classy rig pulled in beside the much smaller black trailer and emerald-green Dodge.

Alfred informed those around him Cora was coming in later. Jake Bob, trying hard not to be rude, continued to peer at Clay. Turning from him Clay concentrated on the navy trailer inscribed with Stuart Stables, Home of Bewick Swan. Roy Scott—chiseled features, dark auburn hair—exited from a matching dually, the passenger's side, with the spring of an in-shape athlete. He heard Terri's quick intact of breath.

"Come on," she said, her voice both strong and curious. "I want to meet Roy Scott."

Clay nodded to Jake Bob and Alfred. "Please excuse us."

She marched right up to him. "My name's Terri Page," she said, a genuine smile on her face. "Green Luck's rider from McDonnell Stables. You must be Roy Scott."

He glanced with disdain at the plain, dust-covered trailer and shrugged.

Clay bit back an expletive.

"You got it," he answered to no one in particular.

Roger Hill, minus his blacksmith's apron, came barreling around the side of the cab and faced them head on. Hiking up his pants, he shook a leg.

"What a long haul," he said displaying a weary grin.

Clay chortled. "I know the feeling."

Jake Bob and Alfred joined them. Martin Riggs had been dispatched to the airport for Cora. Ross Shelton, the scorer, and Marion Gold, the course designer, would be arriving from Connecticut in the morning. The wall and several jumps had been shipped ahead. Tomorrow would be hectic, chaotic, and a test of nerves. The atmosphere began to crackle with electricity.

## Chapter Twelve

Robert Bromwell DVM had to watch it. Jake Bob kept giving him funny looks. Would Cora be suspicious? He found himself acting sneaky. Come on, he lectured. Hold your head up. Act like you own the place.

Leading Green Luck down the spacious aisleway, he automatically checked the stabled slick-coated quarter horses with a vet's eye. Hands milling about gave the giant Irish thoroughbred, draft cross, the once-over. As soon as the horse was settled, he began his search for Alfred.

On the winding path to Jake Bob's huge hacienda, insects buzzed the scattered Texas wildflowers. Old cottonwoods whispered in the breeze. Up ahead on the veranda a *señora* in a colorful skirt and peasant blouse waved. Her pleasant manner made him feel at home as she gave him directions to his room. In turn, he asked where Alfred was staying.

The door was closed. He tapped. No response. Probably lost his hearing aid again, he thought, gently lifting the heavy wrought-iron latch. Slumped in a chair Alfred had his back to him. Robert's heart skipped.

Quickly closing the space between them, he laid his hand on Alfred's shoulder. When Alfred turned to look at him he noticed traces of dried tears on the old man's cheeks. A black-and-white-vintage snapshot rested on his knee.

Alfred coughed, shifting in the tan leather chair. "Green Luck okay?" he asked, discombobulated.

"Green Luck's in great form. It's Terri I need to talk to you about."

Alfred snorted. "Getting bossy, is she?"

"No, no that's not it."

With a faraway look in his eye he fingered the snapshot. "Alice always did before a class. This showdown is in her memory, you know."

Baffled, Robert sat on the hassock at Alfred's feet. *Alice? Memory? What is going on?* "Is that her picture?"

Alfred offered him the snapshot. "Alice, my wife. That's her with Kissy. We were married for two years and two days before she was taken from me."

Robert studied the young woman in flared breeches holding the reins of a gray horse with one hand, a large rosette ribbon in the other. No denying she wore a winner's smile.

Reminiscing more to himself than to Robert, Alfred explained how they'd shown up with an unknown horse and won. Keeping the competition guessing was born that day. Alice had made a game of it. Unabashedly he gazed at Robert.

"She's lovely," Robert said, looking back at the picture. He couldn't trust his voice to say more.

Alfred came forward in the chair and took Robert's hand. "Thank you for playing along with mine and Alice's game. It means a lot to me to end my career like it started, keep 'em guessing and a winner's smile."

A smile so like Terri's. He knew he was caught. No way would he risk fouling up Alfred's elaborate end game. He also knew the chance he'd take if he told Terri. It could backfire in the heat of the moment. Too much pressure. No, he'd keep his oath and remain under the radar screen for one more day.

"No problem," he said, unfolding from the hassock.

Leaving Alfred fondling the snapshot, he went to his room. Slumped on the edge of the bed, he held his head in his hands and prayed Terri would forgive him, the horse would win, Terri would smile—a smile like Alice's—and Alfred found peace.

Alone in the middle of the day Terri normally would've welcomed the time to herself, but when she noticed the unusual rope chair in the hallway, or the Indian painting over the mantel, she wanted to point it out to Robert. She wanted to talk about it. She wanted to call him by his real name. She wanted to hear everything there was to hear about Robert Daniel Brown and his transportation company.

On a quest to find him she left the hacienda and walked back to the arena. The set-up was first class, top-of-the-line, and busy. Inside the arena a crew was removing portable chutes used in rodeo events. The makings of English fences and the hollow blocks for the puissance wall were propped against the barrier separating the bleachers from the sandy arena floor. She watched a florist van unload. Eight huge arrangements were left next to a stack of poles and a heap of cups.

A quiver of excitement raised the hairs on her arms. Leaning against the barrier, she began to burn a visual of entering the ring and flying over the puissance wall. Shaking off tremors, she glanced around for Robert.

Leaving the arena through a side door, she made her way toward the stables. Inside she counted ten stalls on each side of a brick inlayed aisleway. Green Luck, midway and across from a gentlemanly gelding, black with a star, had his nose in a hay bag. Bewick Swan reined supreme in the end stall. His wise eyes peered at her through the bars.

"I ride horses to win," the voice behind her said.

No need to turn around to know it was Roy Scott. "So do I," she said, swallowing a more colorful comeback.

"How come I haven't seen you on the circuit? Don't tell me Alfred has an underground training facility."

Terri had to laugh. "Well put," she said, refusing further information.

"We're going to New Jersey afterwards for an A-rated show," he said rather condescendingly. "It'll be a relief to get this little diversion over with. How about you?"

Little diversion? "Uh, back to Fresno, I believe."

"I'll be working the Swan in the morning around eight."

Terri nodded. "I'll be finished by then."

Jake Bob suggested the evening meeting be held poolside. Terri found Clay at the buffet set up in the mammoth dining room. Together they started for the designated location. The occasional brush of a hip against a thigh quickened her pulse and thumped her heart. Pretending not to be affected, she bit into the apple.

"I saw you pass up the nut-covered brownies," he teased. "The crème-filled doughnuts too."

Terri shrugged and chomped on.

Nudging her elbow, he pointed to the golf cart scooting round the pool edge toward the table and chairs set-up. Cora Stuart—the Cora Stuart—was beside the driver enjoying the ride. Rigid as a ramrod, Martin Riggs sat in the back.

Beside the cart Cora appeared sprightly until the driver handed her a cane. She balanced herself and hobbled forward. She wore a khaki split skirt, a crisp white blouse, and a safari type straw hat. She had the leathered complexion of an outdoors person and the eyes of an alert little bird.

Chairs scraped in the background. In a twinkling, Cora was surrounded by Roy Scott, Roger Hill, and Jake Bob. The crowd parted for Alfred McDonnell.

He gave her a hug and buzzed her cheek. "Well, old gal, are you ready for the Super Bowl? Some wing-dingy, uh."

Her cackle matched his.

The meeting was brief. Basically Alfred wanted to know if anyone had any questions. What he really wanted, Terri suspected, was to feel out the competition. See what they had to say. Roy Scott and Roger Hill remained mum. Cora wanted to know when Marion was arriving and Martin Riggs kept side-glancing Clay.

Terri contributed by asking who was announcing. Alfred gave a snort-cackle and admitted he'd coerced Paul Radley, known as the silver tongue, to do the honors.

Cora edged up to Clay. Leaning on her cane, she furrowed her brows. "You look familiar. Where did Alfred find you?"

"Our paths crossed several years ago. Hauling his horse and rider has been my pleasure."

Masking anxiety, Terri poker-faced it.

Cora frowned. "Alfred's done his best to keep me in the dark. I've never heard of Green Luck, or his rider. Terri Page is it?"

Terri smiled.

Clay chuckled. "He's a piece of work."

After checking with Alfred, Terri and Robert drifted back to the hacienda.

"Too bad you can't be who you are. With all these horse people around, you could pick up all kinds of business."

"Terri, listen. In my case it's not so simple."

She knew he was hiding his past. She felt it. Short of murder, she honestly did not care. "Don't worry," she said, meaning every word. "You passed the test with Cora. The rest is downhill."

Arm around her waist he guided her off the path and into a copse of cottonwoods. His lips brushed against hers. "You're right, Terri. Half-truths are the worst kind. I'm sorry you had to endure the school children's cruelty. And it was cruelty." His lips pressed hers more like a whisper than a kiss. "Sometimes half-truths can't be helped. Look at me," he said, a huskiness to his voice. "I had no idea what I was getting into. Please, forgive me."

"What's . . . what's to forgive?" she murmured leaning into his body. "It was for Alfred. That makes it okay."

He smothered her lips with demanding mastery.

In her room at the hacienda she dug out the alarm clock from her boot, set it for four A.M. Dreamy-eyed, she prepared for bed. Robert was across the hall, two doors down.

So far, so good, Robert deemed. Terri was so close, two doors away. He took a cold shower and jogged back to the stables for a check on Green Luck.

The next morning they met in the hallway, tip-toed down the stairs and to the front door. They paused at the rustle of a skirt behind them.

"*Buenos dias*," the señora whispered. "Here is coffee."

Robert called her a saint. Smiling at the señora's blush, Terri eased on out the door. Robert followed.

It didn't take long to tack Greenie and lead him into the arena. Alfred was waiting for them on the front row of the bleachers. At one point he had Robert put together a practice fence. Terri thanked him with a nod. When Alfred leaned over the barrier, she reined up beside him. Once again he reminded her to give Green Luck a free head and don't sit back on him.

By the time Roy Scott, Cora Stuart, followed by the regal Bewick Swan led by Roger Hill, made a grand entrance into the arena Robert had walked down the Luck and had joined Alfred and Terri in the stands.

Terri observed Cora standing near the barrier chatting with Roger Hill. She didn't seem to be paying much attention to Bewick Swan. Probably doesn't have to, she thought. Somehow that was just as intimidating as Alfred's game. One thing for sure Roy Scott was a master. The Swan's hooves pounding the soft sand matched the heartbeat in her throat. She tensed. Robert discretely covered her hand with his.

Without warning, Alfred left the stands, chit-chatted with Cora at the barrier, and disappeared from sight.

"He's spry this morning," Robert commented.

"Competition turns him on," Terri said, eye on Roy Scott taking the practice fence. "Want to know something?"

"What's that?"

"Roy Scott called the showdown a little diversion. Can you believe it? A *little* diversion."

"He's not letting it get to him," Clay observed.

She flustered. "You think I am?"

His throaty chuckle sent warming shivers throughout her body. Something clicked in her mind. Together they chorused "lighten up." Her face was pink. She felt it.

"Well, we've done it," Robert concluded.

"Uh?"

"We're a team."

Terri smiled. "Come on, I've seen enough."

The walk back to the hacienda was slow and measured. The crisp air, the whispering cottonwoods, the crunch of their boots, and her hand in his began to weave a spell.

"How old are you?"

His question startled her. "Twenty-six. Why?"

At a standstill they looked into each other eyes.

"Hmmm. Just asking"—he brought a handful of her hair to his lips—"I'll be thirty six next month."

Totally confused, she tilted her chin. "So what difference does that make?"

She watched him smile to the heavens above.

"None, I hope."

"Good grief, Robert, I mean Clay, lighten up."

They both laughed.

At the hacienda the buzz around the breakfast buffet centered on that evening. Looking frazzled, Marion Gold, tape measure in the hip pocket of her jeans, picked at the fruit bowl. To no one in particular she said, "I hope Jake Bob's crew sets up the course correctly."

"You mean to your precise specifications," the silver-tongued voice of announcer Paul Radley teased.

Seriously concerned, Marion replied, "They better drag the arena after Jake Bob's quarter horse demonstration, or whatever it is."

Eagle-eyed Ross Shelton, the scorekeeper, joined in. "A big crowd is expected tonight. They'll want to see more than Alfred's one class. I don't have to score Jake Bob's part of the program."

"That's because you don't know a cutting horse

from a billy goat," Paul commented, popping a grape in his mouth.

Giggles and chuckles wafted round the table.

By-passing the dish of oatmeal atop a warming candle and the bowl of fresh fruit, Terri filled her plate with scrambled eggs, sausage patties, and Texas toast. As she spooned gravy on top, she felt Clay's eyes on her. She plopped a doughnut to the side.

"What? You got a problem?"

Robert's frown caught her off guard.

In self defense, she explained, "This is my last meal until it's over. See? There'll be no sugar left to draw water from my muscles. Satisfied?"

Robert quirked a brow. "My, my, my . . ."

"Alfred says I get testy prior to a challenge. Sorry," she apologized, her tone subdued. "I'm going back to bed."

"I understand."

A faint light twinkling in the depths of his silvery, smoky eyes almost changed her mind.

## Chapter Thirteen

The first adrenaline surge occurred at four P.M. Terri found Robert in the stables next to a dun quarter horse in the crossties listening to Jake Bob's trainer explaining the splint on the left front leg. She went straight to Greenie's stall, took a deep breath, and exhaled slowly. Joining her at the stall, Robert waited by her side until she spoke.

"Marion's posting the course," she said, trancelike.

"Then what?"

"I'll burn it in my brain."

Robert edged closer.

She felt his breath on her neck. "I'd better warn you. Once I put on my game face, no distractions."

"Gotcha."

In more ways than one, she thought.

Five o'clock Roy Scott and Terri Page stared at the course posted outside the arena. Robert stood in the background, a program in his hip pocket. Terri stepped back. Behind her hand, she whispered, "I need a magic marker. Rudd packed one in the trunk."

Robert nodded and took off.

Hands shoved down her jeans' pockets, she rocked back on her heels and waited for Cora's rider to join her. "What do you think, Scottie?"

"Nothing the Swan can't handle. The legend lives."

His confidence was unnerving. Intensity lowered her voice. Carefully she measured her words. "Tonight a legend will be born."

He shrugged dismissively.

She bit her lip to stifle a grin.

Shortly after five she'd found a spot under a cottonwood behind the stables. Staring at the magic marked drawing of the course on her left hand, she memorized the twists and turns it'd take to execute a perfect round mandatory prior the wall. Robert sat next to her tapping the folded program atop his knee.

She jabbed him with her elbow. "Look." She pointed to the black slashes. "Round one. Four fences. The distance between the oxer and the vertical is tight."

Cradling her hand in his, he traced his thumb over black lines drawn on her hand. "The Luck can turn on a dime," he said, drawing closer to her.

"Stay focused, Clay Moore."

He released her hand and began counting on his fingers.

"What are you doing?"

"Checking to see how many hours I have left before I can come clean."

The grandfather clock in the corner of the dinning room chimed six times. Hovering over the loaded table, Terri's mouth began to water.

"Got any snack suggestions?"

Robert smiled. "Why don't you try the oatmeal, fruit-filled squares, maybe a diet soda."

"Thanks," she mumbled, placing an oatmeal square on a paper napkin. From a silver tub of ice, she picked out a bottle of spring water.

Backs against the wall and nestled between the clock and a clay pot containing a tall prickly cactus plant, she whispered, "Not the time for a hyper rider."

"Hey, I've given up keeping score."

A ripple of mirth escaped her lips.

The clock chimed the quarter hour. "I'm getting dressed now. Meet you by the stables."

In the bathroom she helped herself to the cotton balls in the Indian pottery bowl on a shelf above the towel rack and scrubbed off the magic marker sketch with fingernail polish remover. The red marks remaining captured her focus. The game face began to take shape.

She spent a long time on her hair, securing the

coppery bun at the nape of her neck. Aware arena
lights had a tendency to wash out her appearance,
she applied make-up heavier than usual. Tonight she
wanted to shine. Sparkle. Look alive. Be brilliant.

In front of the free-standing full-length mirror,
she checked every detail. Looking over her shoulder, she glanced at her behind to make sure no telltale
underwear lines were showing through the snug white
breeches. Satisfied, she stepped back. Eyes narrowed,
concentration at its height, she scoured her brain of no
distractions, no Mrs. Robert Brown, no little Browns
with giant gray eyes.

Touching the edge of her velvet hunt cap with two
fingers, she nodded at her reflection, backed off, and
softly closed the door behind her.

Tripping down the stairs and across a hallway, she
had to pass the great room to get to the door. A white-
haired gentleman in a Western-cut suede jacket that actually smelled of money reached out and nabbed her.
She had no choice but to enter the great room. All eyes
turned to the unknown factor of Alfred's team. After a
few strained moments she politely disengaged herself
from the arm of the suede jacket and headed for the
door. The clock was ticking.

The parking area nearest the arena had filled with
horse trailers belonging to the Fiddle Farm Club
members. Tail gates thudded, horses snorted. Teenage
riders in chaps, Resistols, and sparkly shirts bantered
back and forth. Motion suspended. The comment,

"She must be one of the riders," reached her ears. Smiling, she kept on.

She found Robert behind the stables exercising Green Luck on a long line. Alfred motioned for her to join them. He appeared to be engrossed in the action of his horse.

Wonder when Alfred will tell who he is? Is it a private thing between him and Cora? Side-glancing the spindly octogenarian, she was struck by his countenance. He seemed to be in another world. She'd have to remember to act surprised when he revealed Robert's identity.

Taking a deep breath she turned her attention back to Robert. Robert Daniel Brown. Her stomach tightened. Focus, she told herself. No distractions. Concentrating on her game face, she began to put herself in a zone. Zeroing in on the task at hand she went back in time and recalled a vivid incident of herself and Green Luck.

The wall would be like trail riding in Ireland and coming up on the field stone fence. The fence Greenie cleared. On the way down, they both glimpsed the sheep huddled out of sight at the base. She could still feel Green Luck's belly roll mid-air to prevent landing atop the startled animals. The next day they took a similar stone fence. Greenie did not balk. Blind trust. They had it.

"Bring him in," Alfred called.

Jarred out of reverie, she blinked.

Leading Green Luck, Robert joined them.

On the way to the stalls Alfred stopped at the back side of an empty trailer. Huddling together he made his final statement, "Don't sit back, give the horse his head. Let him fly."

Terri nodded. Robert asked if he had any instructions for him. Alfred crammed his gnarled hand into the pocket of his windbreaker and brought forth several sugar cubes.

"Here," he said, handing the cubes to Robert. "Give him one for good measure. He'll need a shot of energy."

Terri couldn't look at Robert. The rumbles of silly, nervous giggles were building and the last thing she wanted to do was set them off. She heard Robert clear his throat. It sounded jerky.

Martin Riggs caught up with them as they entered the shadowy aisleway. A staff member flipped the light switch.

"There you are, Alfred," Martin said, trying to hide a flutter of nervousness. "I've been looking all over for you. By the way, so is the media."

As if on cue, a reporter and a cameraman, TV call letters on their jackets, entered the wide door and made a beeline for them.

"Evening Mr. McDonnell," the reporter said, eyeing Terri for all he was worth.

Acknowledging the intrusion, Alfred nodded.

Terri recognized the man. He looked heavier and

taller on TV. His sprayed-stiff hair appeared a little too blond. Unconsciously, she drew in her stomach muscles, straightened her shoulders. Robert quietly transposed himself to the far side of Martin Riggs.

"We're doing a feature of this, this shootout"—he chuckled—"for our Horse Doings segment. I'd like to interview your rider."

"My pleasure." Alfred stepped aside.

Robert inched further away. Back turned, he became intensely interested in the stabled mare next to Green Luck.

The camera light beamed on Terri.

The reporter took on a TV voice. "After years of bringing excitement to the equestrian world Alfred McDonnell and Cora Stuart are finally going head to head, one on one tonight. Is that correct?" He stuck the mike under her chin.

"Yes. The puissance wall is devoted to the theory that horses can fly and that's what it's all about."

Retrieving the mike, the reporter asked, "And can you tell me which horse is going to fly the highest tonight?" Again he shoved the microphone under her chin.

"The best horse, of course," she said brightly.

"And which horse is that?" he persisted.

"Green Luck! Who else?"

Cutting the mike, the reporter laughed. "Well said. Off the record, we all know McDonnell Stables' motto. Is that why I haven't seen you before?"

"Something like that," she hedged.

"I couldn't believe Roger Hill is Scottie's assis-tant."

"He's a topnotch farrier."

"And who is yours?"

Robert appeared from around the side of Martin. Extending a hand, he said, "Moore. Clay Moore."

Accepting the hand, he peered into his face. "You look just like Robert—"

## Chapter Fourteen

Terri muffled a dramatic groan. Puzzled, the reporter shifted his attention to her.

Maneuvering around the TV guys, Robert faced Terri. "What's wrong?" he asked, eyes focused on hers.

"I forgot it," she moaned.

"Forgot what?"

She gave a dramatic sigh. "My good luck girth. It's on the floor in my room. I hate to ask, but would you mind?"

Saved by the ruse, he winked and, with a sigh of relief, took off in a run.

Distracted by Scottie on Bewick Swan followed by a gaggle of Fiddle Farm teenagers passing in front of the wide doors, the TV crew disappeared after them.

When the dust settled, Martin asked Alfred if he was ready to leave.

Terri touched his arm. "Any last words?" she asked, trying to keep the urgency out of her voice.

Alfred wore a deadpan expression. He spoke slowly. "Don't mount Green Luck until the end of Jake Bob's part. During intermission and while the course is being set, take a few practice fences. Marion's set them up by the parking lot. Save his energy for the big one."

"Okay." She gave his arm a little squeeze.

On their way out of the stables, Martin glanced over his shoulder and gave her a thumbs up.

Leaning against the stall, she waited for Robert's return. Martin is suspicious. I feel it. Why is it everyone knows him except me? I mean he's hiding from Cora, Jake Bob, the reporter. The reporter, she pondered. What's the connection there? How come a horse hauler knows him? We wouldn't be having this cat-and-mouse game if the truth were known. As long as he isn't a trainer . . .

She watched him approach, a working girth slung over his shoulder and not one she'd use. He'd confiscated the ball cap, Just Jump It across the front, from the chair where she'd left it. Pulled down low on his forehead the brim touched the top of the funky Hally Trick glasses. For good measure he faked a hitch to his gait.

She wanted to giggle. *He looks like a dork.* "Thanks," she muffled and moved aside from the tack box.

Clay placed the girth on the lid. "I was afraid your interviewer was going to spill the beans."

"How did you know him?"

"I told you. I've been in a lot of barns."

Terri's brows furrowed. So had the reporter, she thought. Why would he remember a drifter? Or had it been a recent encounter with the horse transportation business? Shrugging off the jag of puzzlement, she glanced at the round clock above the wash stall.

The red lines atop her hand were faint now. Before they disappeared completely she studied the pattern of the fences. By her side Robert remained silent. When the snap, crackle and testing one-two-three of the PA system could be heard, she said, "Let's go outside. I need to know when the Fiddle Farm Club exhibition winds down. That's when we tack Green Luck."

Terri scoped the location of the practice fence. Satisfied, she turned to Robert. He'd tipped back the cap. The black-framed glasses were tucked in his shirt pocket. His silvery-gray eyes devoured her.

She had to look away. "Clay. Robert. Whoever. How's all this going to end?"

He slipped his arm around her shoulder. "You'll find out at the celebration party. I hope you'll forgive me."

"What is that supposed to mean?"

Before he could answer Paul Radley's voice sallied forth from the voluminous building. "Welcome to Jake Bob Johnson's Arena. We are here tonight to witness—"

"I gotta concentrate," she said.

He couldn't bear to think about it. At least Cora and Alfred hadn't timed the event. Their rules were simple. If you clear the four fences, you get a shot at the wall. If you cleared the wall, blocks would be added on. The horse flying the highest would win.

He admired her nerve. In his opinion that's what it'd take. She knows Green Luck emotionally and physically. He kept telling himself Greenie would provide the athletic effort, she, the brains and verve to guide the horse. He'd seen the mandatory ambulance parked nearby.

From a distance she looked like a brave soldier preparing for battle. He wanted to go to her. Hold her. Tell her about Alice, the oath, how his hands got tied. Pressure mounting, he felt uneasy. He wasn't out of the woods yet.

The splashy orange and pink Texas sunset, the strategically placed spotlights bathed the area around the stables and the back entrance to the arena in an unreal lighting. The Fiddle Farm Club members, flags in hand, were lined up on prancing Western horses ready to go in. The show was on. His skin prickled.

Leaning against the hitching rail beside the stable, Terri fumed. "Scottie's a pain."

Clay chuckled. "What do you mean?"

"He's been trying to get me shook."

Concerned, he faced her. "Trash talking?"

"No, no. Not that. Just little digs here and there."

He took her hand. "Don't let it bother you."

She grinned up at him. "Actually, he did me a favor. Now I'm more determined than ever."

He couldn't deny the competitor's glint in her eye.

The gaily-tacked horses gathered at the back entrance to the arena provided a distraction to help pass the time. They began to make comments on the ones they liked, the ones they didn't. All was going smoothly until Roger Hill led the mighty Bewick Swan out the stable and to the practice fence. Roy Scott mounted, trotted, cantered, and cleared the fence.

"Okay, now where are we?" she asked, gravity in her tone. "Have you been keeping up with the schedule?"

"Yes, ma'am. Next to the last class. As soon as the working Western horses go in, I'll get Green Luck."

Side by side, arms touching, he could feel her muscles tense. Softly, he whispered, "Take a deep breath."

Terri moved away from him.

At the practice fence Green Luck did a fair amount of prancing, making sure everyone saw him before Terri took charge. The fence was a piece of cake bringing the moment of truth nearer. Robert stretched and concentrated on relaxing.

He watched the tractor, blade attached to the front end, enter the ring. A pickup loaded with fence makings and giant baskets of flowers pulled up.

Marion jumped out of the truck and paced beside the vehicle.

"Anything you want me do?" he asked, studying her eyes.

"Be ready," she replied, her face set in determination.

In rare form Paul Radley's rich tenor voice announced, "And now, ladies and gentlemen, what we've all been waiting for. After years of filling the stands at Devon, Palm Beach, Spruce Meadows, Cora Stuart and Alfred McDonnell are going head to head. Tonight we are privileged to—"

At the back entrance to the arena, Terri dismounted and handed the reins to Robert. Beside her Scottie adjusted his collar. At the signal both entered the ring to walk the course. To this crowd Roy Scott was as familiar as could be. Terri was not. She was the new kid on the block.

Robert smiled at the determination in her steps as she mentally counted the strides between the fences. Keeping his emotions in check, he fought the urge to rush out there to be by her side. Will this contest ever end?

Ross Shelton met them at the gate for the coin toss. From the laughter on her face and the elbow jab to Scottie's arm, he could tell that she'd won. He knew she wanted to go last.

Both mounted at the gate. Terri gave Scottie ample

room. A hush descended throughout the arena. Paul
Radley started in with Roy Scott's traditional bio of
his grand prix career, beginning at age seventeen when
he placed second in his first major jumping event.
Next he listed his many wins over the years.

Robert clamped his hand over her boot. Terri
leaned forward in the saddle. He watched her concentrate on Scottie's round. Soon the pounding of hooves
picked up speed. Over the five-foot nine-inch vertical
fence they sailed. He could hear her counting the
strides to the next one, a six-foot spread. A tight turn
and Bewick Swan faced a four-foot six-inch fence,
and on to the last obstacle, a five-foot spread. Scottie,
patting the Swan's neck, exited at the gate. Applause
erupted.

Eyes straight ahead, Terri entered the ring. Paul's in-
troduction included a bare bones sketch of her career.
He mentioned training in Ireland and cracked a keep
'em guessing joke in reference to Alfred. The English
equestrian crowd loved it. Robert's heart landed in his
throat.

Marion's wealth of knowledge had done a good job
designing a course to fit the arena. Dead center the
puissance wall of gray-painted hollow blocks rose up
like a monster from the depths. Giant flower arrangements flanked each side. The four fences were strategically, yet cleverly, placed on the sides.

*She looks controlled and collected,* he thought as

she took the first fence. The scene playing out in front of him seemed to be taking place in slow motion. He didn't realize he was holding his breath until she was safely over the last obstacle. Grinning, he met her at the gate. Face flushed, she looked down at him from the height of the horse.

Behind them the pickup appeared with two of Jake Bob's crew hunkered in the bed. Moving aside, they let them through to remove all but one fence, giving the riders a long approach to the wall.

"Riders are given the option for a warm-up fence before tackling the wall and . . ." Paul was saying. Robert checked the girth one more time.

Spellbound, he watched Scottie enter the ring and take the fence before turning to face the test. His thoughts ran rampant. What was Alfred thinking? They're as professional as you can get.

Roy Scott's success clearing the wall brought a round of applause. Robert sought eye contact with Terri. Her expression told him she was thinking along the same lines.

She entered the ring at a full gallop and headed straight for the wall. A collective, suspended gasp hung in the air. Green Luck started his ascent. At the top, knees tucked, hind legs under him, he executed a move that defied anything he'd ever seen. The twist resembled a belly roll.

Stunned, the paralyzed spectators paused before

they applauded the horse's extraordinary athleticism. Robert ran to the gate to meet her.

"Are you okay?" he croaked, throat clogged in tension.

Grinning from ear to ear, she did not answer.

The crew ran in to heighten the wall. Standing at six feet nine inches, it looked insurmountable to the naked eye.

Roy Scott entered the ring for a shot at the heightened wall. Not to be out done by Terri, he skipped the warm up fence and headed straight for the wall.

The master in the irons did everything by the book. It didn't help. Bewick Swan's hind hoof touched the top. It seemed an eternity before two blocks toppled to the floor of the arena. Groans rose up from the spectators.

Robert checked Green Luck's girth, adjusted the bridle, and asked if she needed anything. Jaws clamped, she shook her head and waited for the crew members to reset the blocks.

He couldn't stand it. The suspense was beyond him. "I love you," slipped from his lips. Out the tail end of his eye, he caught her expression, one that was in a different zone. He wasn't at all sure if she'd heard him, or comprehended what he'd declared.

Once more she entered the ring at a gallop. At the take-off point, she threw the reins practically over Greenie's head and let him go. The horse sailed upwards, twisted at the top, and came down on an angle. Every block remained intact. Paul's declaring her the winner was nearly lost over the crowd's spontaneous reaction.

Pandemonium broke out.

Robert tossed the ball cap in the air.

His cell phone beeped.

## Chapter Fifteen

Fist pumping, Terri took a victory lap. It was all so unreal and, with the pressure off, she had to force herself to pay attention to the movements of Green Luck. *Did he say he loved me? Did I hear that, or did I imagine it*, she breathed to herself.

After the cheering lap she brought the horse to a halt beside Scottie, who was mounted on Bewick Swan stationed in the middle of the ring.

"Congratulations," he said.

Through a smile she couldn't contain, she murmured, "Thanks. Whew!"

The spectators spilled out into the arena, the media leading the way. Like the Red Sea parting, they separated providing a passageway for Cora and Alfred.

Terri couldn't keep her eyes off Alfred's shuffle

beside Cora's cane-thumping measured steps, both making their way to the horses. Alfred placed his hand on Green Luck's shoulder. Gazing up at her, he had the look of anticipation on his face.

She gave him a smile. A smile of victory, adoration, and love for him and for Robert all mixed into one. Alfred, salty moisture glistening his cheeks, trembled. Terri sailed off Greenie and took him in her arms. "We did it," she said, tears in her own eyes.

He held on to her for a few seconds and then, without a word, signaled for her to get back on the horse.

Jake Bob elbowed his way through to them. Hoisting a championship-engraved silver bowl over his head, he sidled up to Alfred. Paul Radley's tenor voice took over. It was an exciting moment, but she couldn't really comprehend what was being said about her amazing feat over the wall. Instead, she stood in the stirrups to search the crowd for Robert.

Without warning the bright yellow beam of the TV camera was on her, the mike thrust upward.

"Congratulations!"

She nodded.

"Tell us about that spectacular move over the wall."

"I owe everything I know to Alfred's trainer, Wayne Rudd."

"If Rudd's on Alfred's payroll, it must be a secret!"

Terri couldn't help but laugh. She wanted so badly to tell Clay, now, Robert Brown, what really happened. Twisting in the saddle, she scanned the crowd. Where is he?

The crowd began to break off into little groups. Radley announced a celebration party at Jake Bob's. Roger Hill appeared beside Bewick Swan and Roy Scott. They began to make their way towards the gate leading out of the arena. Trying not to be obtrusive, Terri glanced around for Robert. Feeling deserted, she started out on her own. Without warning, a member of Jake Bob's staff materialized by her side.

"Clay Moore asked me to tell you he had an emergency. He'll call you first chance," he said, falling into step beside her. "I'll take care of your horse for you."

"What emergency?" she asked, staring down at the lanky cowboy in a cattle-creased Resistol.

"He didn't say, ma'am."

Emotions roiled within her. Why now? What is going on?

Knees trembling, she dismounted outside the arena and handed the reins to the cowboy. "When did this happen?"

"Right after you did that wall. He came running up to me and asked for my help. He said he had to go to Dallas right away. It was an emergency."

Terri followed him into the stables and watched as he handled the horse. From the show trunk, she retrieved a halter and a jar of liniment.

"He needs to be walked down before you put him

up. This"—she handed him the jar—"goes on his legs."

"Yes, ma'am. That's what Clay Moore said to do."

Satisfied Green Luck was in good hands, she started for the hacienda and the celebration party. She hadn't gone far when she spotted Alfred up ahead with Paul and Martin Riggs. Under normal circumstances she would've run to catch up. Now she wanted to be alone to sort out her feelings. Mainly to ponder if she'd heard Robert correctly, or did she imagine it. I love you. Was her subconscious playing tricks? What kind of emergency? Why didn't he say good-bye?

A gathering spread from the dining area to the great room. Glasses tinkled, chatter echoed. Avoiding contact, she headed up the stairs to her room to change. A party was the last thing on her mind, but she owed Alfred that much. It was his night.

Two doors down, she noticed the wedge of light coming from Robert's partially opened door. Intrigued, she approached his room, paused, and entered. The duffle bag was gone. An eerie feeling of being where she shouldn't be came over her. Taking one last glance, she stopped cold. There it was. The briefcase propped against the nightstand. For reasons she didn't understand she picked it up and took it to her room.

*He might want me to check something for him when he calls,* she told herself placing the briefcase on the bed.

She tugged off the English boots. Stripped of her

riding habit she washed off the make-up, arranged her hair, and dressed in jeans and a pale-blue oxford shirt. All the while the briefcase remained on the bed, pulling her like a magnet.

On the floor, back against the bedstead, she held the cell phone in her hand. "Call," she said to the phone. "I can't wait much longer. Alfred needs me downstairs."

She glanced at her watch. *Okay. Five minutes and counting, that's all you get, Robert Daniel Brown. Bad as I want to know what's going on, I'd rather take your phone call in privacy than in the middle of the party downstairs. Was the emergency so bad you couldn't wait to say good-bye?*

She tried to ignore the briefcase on the bed. Drumming her fingers on her kneecaps, she frowned. Finally she told herself she'd be prepared with any information he might need when he calls. It'll save time. Reaching over her head, she tugged the case onto her lap.

Tamping down the feeling that she was invading his privacy, she popped the lid. The first manila folder contained a medical history of a horse. Puzzled, she scanned the information. This belongs to Doctor Robert Bromwell, that famous veterinarian. How did he get that? Inside the next folder was an engineer-type sketch. What is this? Frowning, she figured it was a hydraulic design for . . . something. It made no sense.

Underneath she picked up the slim volume of *Ten Tips to Conquer Colic* and smiled. *I've heard of this book. Rudd swears by it. I guess Robert keeps it on hand in case he has a problem. Well, he sure did know what to do when Greenie had an attack.*

Keeping the briefcase contents in order she turned the book over, placed it on top of the folders, and was about to dig further when her eye caught the portrait on the back of the book. Brows furrowed, she picked up the book again. There's something familiar about him.

She gulped. Air caught in her throat. She brought the portrait close to her face. Robert Daniel Bromwell DVM printed beneath stunned her senses. The sandy hair, the gray eyes, the quirky little smile left no doubt.

Shock kept her momentarily immobilized, but nothing prepared her for the title printed on the next folder, "Can Diet Affect Peak Performance During Stressful Competition? Subject: Terri Page." Perspiration beaded her forehead. Her hands trembled. Cautiously, she opened the folder.

Torn from a medical journal was an article on hyperactivity in athletes. Jotted in the margin were notes scribbled in his handwriting. The next page, formatted like a diary, contained a detailed account of what she'd eaten starting with the peanut butter and jelly sandwich and candy bar, the first night. She gaped at his comments on her reaction from the doughnuts consumed at the farewell party.

Several sheets of paper the size of the notepad he'd kept in his shirt pocket slipped out. She read in disbelief. A list of her vitamins prompted a quick flashback. Returning from the garage after paying a visit to the washer, she'd eased inside. With his back to her he was jotting notes. The light was on in the bathroom, the cabinet door hung by a hinge. That dirty rotten sneak! How could he do this?

She snapped shut the briefcase and tossed it aside. Arms folded around her knees, she buried her face. Each piece of her broken heart brought enormous pain, humiliation, anger, and hurt. *Use me, that's all he had in mind. Use me for his stupid research. I hope he's satisfied, the coward. Emergency my as . . . astronomical behind. He couldn't face me. Of all the injustices in the world, being used is the worst. I'm sick of it.*

*He could've trusted me with the truth if he'd wanted to. No. He was having too much fun yanking my chain.* Robert Brown. Robert Daniel Brown. Alfred McDonnell pulled a good one. Not his fault. Tears gathered. *Not his fault at all. He was going for a complete surprise to Cora. I was the one who got the bombshell.*

*Love me?* She choked. *That was my imagination, that's what I wanted to hear.* The sobbing began.

## Chapter Sixteen

Robert Bromwell tossed the cap, yelled a yahoo, and danced a little jig. She did it! He started for the gate. Two strides and his cell phone beeped. Stopped in his tracks, he muttered an expletive. Tony Eakin was privy to his number, but only if it was a life or death matter. He ducked behind the wide doors. Outside, he was alone.

"Yes?" he answered.

"Old Man Coleman's stud fractured a cannon bone."

"How'd it happen?"

"Freak deal. Stepped in a fence hole."

Of all times. "What about the rays?"

Tony fired off like an M-16.

"Encase the leg in plaster. Supports are in the closet.

If you can't find them call Tracy. Get the paramedic at the firehouse to give you a hand."

"That's not the problem."

"What do you mean?"

"Old Man Coleman doesn't want me to touch the horse. He wants you."

Robert frowned. *Not now, not when I want to be with Terri. Tony can handle it. Standard procedure.*

"Are you there?"

"Can't you take care of it?"

Tony's voice faltered. "The horse I can handle. It's Miss Angie that's got me worried. She's afraid her husband is liable to suffer heart failure if you don't get here."

Robert frowned. *The man's obsessed with the horse.* He was running a clinic not a hand-holding service. Tony could take care of it. He knew it was ludicrous to compare Coleman to the night Cory was hooked. It had happened so fast. He couldn't help it and he found himself saying, "I'm on my way."

Decision made, he ran back to the gate. One glance at the crowd surrounding her and he knew it was hopeless. Nabbing one of Jake Bob's cowboys, he asked him to look after Green Luck and took off. In his room he grabbed his shaving kit, shoved it in the duffle bag. Without a backward glance he headed for the pickup. Spinning wheels, he was on his way.

Not five miles down the lonely road he regretted

his decision. Not one to go back on his word, he knew he couldn't turn around. All the while he berated himself for having to be there for the clinic.

He yanked off the glasses, lowered the window and threw them out into the darkness as if that would vindicate him from the charade. His eyes watered; his heart physically ached. *Please,* he prayed, *don't let her hate me for this.* He hit the map light, held the phone under it, and punched in her number. She answered on the fourth ring.

"Well, well, well," she said in a huffy manner, "If it isn't the famous Robert Daniel Bromwell DVM."

"Look, Ter—"

"You look! I congratulate you on your *research.* Just think. You can write another book on eating habits of riders. Tip one, no doughnuts."

His stomach hit bottom. She'd been in the briefcase. "There's more to this than—"

"Gotta go." Her voice cracked.

"Terri, listen. About the research. Read all of it."

"What? Digest the brilliant dissertation by the famous Doctor Bromwell? Not a chance!" She cut him off.

Trembling, she stood there, phone in hand. In a fit she threw the instrument on the bed. It bounced off the briefcase. She couldn't believe the emotions tearing through her body.

*Tap. Tap. Tap.*

Pulling herself together, she croaked, "Yes?"

*Tap. Tap. Tap.*

Cracking the door, she repeated, "Yes?"

The señora smiled. "You're wanted downstairs, *por favor.*"

"Thank you. Soon as I fix my hair," she said, closing the door as she spoke.

Later she'd worry what had come over her, but at the moment it made perfect sense. This was Alfred's last wing-dingy. She'd make it memorable, a tribute to the best horseman in the world. Her only regret was that Wayne Rudd was not here to witness it.

She started by undoing the classic bun at the nape of her neck and piling the golden-red tresses atop her head. Holding them in place with one hand, she dug in her canvas bag with the other for a packet of mane braid rubber bands. In the bathroom she pulled her hair through the band. Carefully she loosened several tendrils for a softening affect. Foundation, lipstick, and a touch of blush was applied, the mascara creatively, in record speed.

She fumbled with the oxford shirt buttons, whipped it off, and threw it on the bed. Next she found the silk pale-blue top in her luggage, shook it out, and slipped it on. Wiggling out of her jeans, she kicked them across the floor. No time for knee-highs or pantyhose. The black crepe slacks slid on like butter on a hot corn cob. She stepped in a pair of sandals as she hurried out the door.

At the top of the stairs she took a deep breath,

held her head high. Right on, she said to herself and marched down the steps. In the hallway to the left a few guests were milling around the buffet table, to the right, a jam-packed great room. Someone spotted her.

"There she is!"

All eyes trained on her. Shoulders pulled back, she entered the great room and needled her way through the crowd to Alfred's side. Before she could speak, Martin Riggs in his courtroom voice commanded the attention of everyone present.

"This night signifies the ending of Alfred McDonnell's and Cora Stuart's careers. We are all indebted to them for their ability to fill the stands, promote the circuit, and for being responsible for many of our generous sponsors to come onboard. We are truly grateful for such monumental contributions."

Applause erupted. Terri smiled at Alfred.

"We will miss our compatriots . . ."

Terri held on to Alfred's arm.

". . . however, ladies and gentleman, did you truly expect Alfred to go out in any other way except by his trademark?"

Laughter.

"I trust no one had seen the mighty Green Luck or his rider, Terri Page, but who recognized the groom?"

People began to exchange puzzled looks. Terri's whole body tightened. She wanted to run.

"Who but Alfred McDonnell could complete the team of horse, rider, and groom in complete secrecy?

Did anyone recognize Clay Moore as Doctor Robert Bromwell?"

The revelation prompted a collective gasp. A hearty round of hand clapping broke out punctuated by a few "woo woo's" Alfred cackled and cackled. Cora came to his side. "You old scoundrel," she said, still in shock. Alfred's cackling was contagious. She had to join in.

Martin Riggs wasn't finished. "This will go down in the archives of equestrian history. However, as we all know, the buzz is the exceptionally athletic move by Green Luck. Would Alfred care to comment?"

Knowing he didn't have a clue, Terri stepped forward. "One day while across the pond," she began in a tone she didn't recognize, "Green Luck and I were trail riding when we came upon a fence made of field stone." Her voice became animated as she picked up steam. "Actually, the fence looked a heck of a lot like the wall." She let that sink it.

"We had a choice. Take the fence or find a gate, and I have to tell you, they're not much on gates over there. Well, midway Greenie caught sight of a pair of sheep huddled at the base. He twisted his body to avoid landing on them."

She had their attention. You could hear a pin drop.

"Marion's beautiful flower arrangements on each side of the wall cast a similar shadow at the base. Greenie took one look, thought sheep, and did his move!"

She could hear Alfred's snort-cackle.

"What I'd like to know," she continued, searching

for eye contact with her opponent, "is Scottie's take on the shadow."

Tipsy Scottie, hanging on to the sideboard loaded with amber bottles of spirits, called out, "How do like that? Bested by a pair of fake sheep!"

Good-will laughter exploded. The room rocked. Terri couldn't help but join in. Speech over, she caught up with Alfred and Cora. The attention and the excitement kept her on a dreamlike high. She knew when she crashed the hurt of a broken heart would be unbearable. She had to gather strength. Get over it.

The party continued on until the wee hours. The gentleman in the money-smelling suede jacket latched on to her. Smiling and smiling until her cheeks nearly cracked she felt a schizophrenic split taking place. One half wore a party face mask. The other half, the one underneath, smoldered dark with pain.

Alfred held in there as long as he could. When he left she soon followed and began the trek up the dark and lonely stairs. Someone had turned off the light in Robert's room. At her door she paused, drew a ragged breath.

On the edge of the bed she collapsed, completely depleted. She felt a wretchedness come over her. It hurt. Assailed by a terrible sense of confusion, she couldn't understand why she attracted guys who couldn't abide by the truth.

What is wrong with me? She wailed, kicking off a sandal. *Am I so gullible "the Robert Bromwell"*

*thinks he can do what he wants, say what he pleases?
How can I have feelings for anyone who doesn't ap-
preciate the pure and simple truth? If he'd cared for
me he could have told me who he was. No, he was too
interested in his research. All that team stuff was an
act. He was an act and I fell for it.* Deep sobs racked
her insides. Tears gushed down her cheeks.

She wanted to go to McDonnell Stables, be with
Rudd and Maggie, Rick, and the gang. Families don't
run off. They stick by you no matter what.

The next morning she'd packed before she went
downstairs. She was on a mission. Alfred was nowhere
in sight, and having no idea what his plans were, she
searched for Martin Riggs. She found him on the veranda drinking coffee with Marion. He and Alfred,
he told her, were staying on a few days. Luckily she
would be able to hitch a ride to the airport with Marion. Alfred appeared at the last moment, giving her a
chance to share her plans. Bad as she wanted to know,
she did not ask who'd be hauling Green Luck back to
Fresno.

The ride to the Dallas-Fort Worth Airport with Marion was provided by a cowhand from Jake Bob's outfit.
While "You Are My Sunshine" hammered round and
round in her head, she worried about Robert's briefcase. Maybe she shouldn't have taken it with her.

"I've designed many courses," Marion said, "and
never had a shadow complaint."

Terri giggled. "I knew what Greenie was thinking."

"If you ask me," the cowhand opined, "that kind of jumping pushes the horse. I believe in working them."

Marion and Terri remained tight-lipped.

The two hour wait in the airport lowered her spirits to the point of depression. To make matters worse security confiscated a hoof pick, a holepuncher, and a pair of scissors from her backpack. Trying hard to cope, she focused on Rudd and Maggie meeting the plane in Fresno.

The long flight encouraged memories of Robert hauling the horse, telling her to lighten up, and the night in Flagstaff sleeping in his arms. The comfort, the strength, the long, lingering kiss . . . she sucked in.

Turning to the elderly passenger next to her, she made small talk and, for the rest of the flight, she learned more than she cared to know about her six grandchildren. Mercy, she thought, rubbing her temples, will this flight ever end.

At last the plane banked. Snapping the seatbelt, she chomped at the bit. The first passenger to stand, she waited impatiently for the crew to roll the stairs to the door. On the artificially lit tarmac, she looked toward the airport facility. Through the plate glass wall, she spied Rudd and Maggie. She took off in a sprint. She grabbed Wayne Rudd first, gave him a hug. Maggie's outstretched arms and warm smile prompted a dive into them.

"Man, I missed you guys," she said, grinning.

"Have you eaten?" Maggie asked.

Terri shrugged. "I don't remember. I don't even know what time it is!"

"I've got leftovers. You look a little peaked."

Leftovers at Rudd's was not the usual fried chicken, salad sprinkled with crispy bacon crumbles, the rich pecan pie. Maggie apologized for the skinless baked turkey breast, the tasteless, greaseless gravy, and soft mushy vegetables. "Wayne's diet, you know."

Terri nodded.

Antsy, Rudd watched each bite slip down her throat. When he couldn't stand it any longer he started in on the questions. Terri obliged with every detail she could think of, from the colic in Flagstaff to the bra snatching in Albuquerque. She described the wonderful family in Amarillo, the tight quarters in Dallas.

At last she got to Jake Bob's arena. Martin had told him about Green Luck's belly twist, but she had to recount it from the very beginning, stride by stride. They loved Scottie's remark, secretly savoring his defeat.

They discussed Bewick Swan and Roy Scott. Both agreed he was a master in the irons, but Green Luck had the advantage. Finally he brought up the part she'd been dreading.

"I didn't find out Clay Moore was Doc Bromwell until Martin called with the results. That's amazing. I don't see how Alfred talked him into it."

Terri propped her elbows on the table and cradled

her chin in her hands. "Robert said he owed Alfred a big one."

"Oh, I know what that was. Alfred was the first one to let him try an unproven procedure on his gelding, Nodden. That's what started Doc's career."

Her head throbbed. She wanted off the subject. When Rudd paused, she asked how Rick was.

Surprise crossed his face. "You haven't heard?"

"Heard what?"

"Alfred's turning the stables over to the state for a park. Courier's been sold to Hamilton Farms in Virginia. Rick has agreed to go with the horse. Tell you the truth, that was a lucky break for him."

Terri blanched.

Maggie looked concerned. "Terri, you've got to be worn out. This can continue tomorrow. I might as well warn you. Your phone is going to be ringing off the hook with offers."

Rudd looked like he was going to burst. "We got one. Stuart Stables has been turned over to Kristin. We're going to New York day after tomorrow to check it out."

Mind reeling with the quickness of the change of events, she had to ask if he knew Green Luck's fate.

Rudd shook his head. "When Alfred didn't make arrangements for Greenie to come back here, I figured he'd been sold too."

"Man, this is happening so fast."

The following afternoon Terri was still in bed in a

deep state of slumber until the phone ringing jarred her awake. Groggy, she groped for the instrument.

"This is Frederick Stables in North Carolina," the southern voice drawled. "Congratulations! It's the talk of the circuit. What I'd like to offer is a job here in the Tar Heel State."

Slumped on the bed, she tried to concentrate. "I'll keep it in mind," she said. "I'm not sure of my plans."

And so the afternoon went just as Maggie had predicted. Her standard answer was I'll get back with you and scratched the number on the back of an envelope. When her cell phone beeped, she checked the digital screen, recognized Robert's number, and punched the power-off button.

The activity at the stables centered around the boarders being picked up by owners, leased horses dealt with, and Alfred's sale horses poured over by excited buyers. Grand Central on this sunny Fresno afternoon. What was left of the staff huddled in amazement at the commotion taking place.

The next day proved to be a rerun. Terri pitched in, but it wasn't the same. Rick was gone and Rudd had his mind on New York. One by one, riders, grooms, stable hands were absorbed by other facilities. She felt hollow on the inside.

Back in the apartment she wondered if she should be packing. Packing to go where? The North Carolina deal sounded good. Not as many benefits as McDonnell Stables, but it seemed like the best bet.

Hoping Alfred would soon return, she wanted to go over the list with him.

Despite keeping busy, thoughts of Robert intruded. His name lingered around the edges of her mind during the day, driving her crazy. Nights were spent shaking off memories of another time.

## Chapter Seventeen

Late the following night, a clump on the stairs jarred her from an uneasy sleep. Cautiously peeling back the covers she sat up. Silence. What was that? She frowned. The clumping started up again. This time accompanied by a magical voice. A voice so deep and melodious it sent quivers up her spine.

"You are my sunshine, my only sunshine."

Her heart pounded in her ears.

"You make me happy when skies are gray. You'll never know dear—"

*I may be gullible, but I'm not stupid.* Pulse racing, she groped the foot of the bed until she made contact with her sweatshirt and pants.

"—how much I love you."

*I'm going to throw that briefcase right in his face.*

195

"Please don't take my sunshine away."

Robert Bromwell lightly tapped on the door. She pulled on the sweatpants and struggled with the sweatshirt over her long T-shirt. Legs swung over the side of the bed, she held her head.

He tapped louder.

She flicked on the table lamp. On her way to take care of the matter, she latched on to the briefcase propped against the brown chair.

The knob squeaked. She shoved the case through a wedge opening. Even in the darkness the faint glow of the table lamp was enough. His bleary eyes pleaded with her. She opened the door wider. The black luscious hair above the sandy roots hadn't been combed. He needed a shave.

A second passed before she realized he was handing her a crumbled box of doughnuts. She thrust the briefcase forward. He accepted with a nod.

"May I come in? I have something I want you to see."

Despite every effort to cut him off, curiosity set in. "Uh, uh," she muttered, floundering for something more appropriate.

He had his foot in the door. Slipping past her, he stumbled over a mountain of laundry. At the bed he sank to the floor and reached over his head for a pillow.

"First I have to tell you about Alice."

She glared down at him.

"Please," he said, patting a place beside him, "give me a chance. This concerns Alfred."

The magic words, she had no choice.

"I swore to Alfred I wouldn't reveal my identity. That was before I met you. If Little Justin hadn't interrupted, I would've washed off the eye stuff and—"

"What's Alice got to do with Alfred?"

He sighed. "I'm trying to tell you."

He looked wiped out, ready to collapse. Her voice softened. "I'm listening."

"That night I called Alfred to beg off, but he lost his hearing aid in the middle of the conversation."

A nervous giggle escaped. Quickly she regained composure.

He fumbled with the box top. "Doughnut?"

Every fiber wanted him to continue. "How about coffee?"

"Soda, if you have it."

At the apartment-size refrigerator she got one for him and one for herself. Back on the floor by his side she plucked a doughnut from the box. Their fingertips brushed.

"I missed you," he mumbled.

"Go on," she said weakly.

"Clay Manure"—he shook his head—"caught me off guard. I got as far as Robert. If those riders hadn't been hanging on to every word I would've come clean. You know how stable gossip is. I'm glad I didn't because of Alice."

"What's Alice got to do with it?" she demanded, more confused than ever.

"Alice," he said, reaching out for her hand, "was Alfred's wife. She's the one responsible for his trademark."

His touch sent a signal she tried to ignore.

"As soon as we got to Fiddle, I tracked down Alfred. I found him in his room. He was looking at an old snapshot. Before I could ask to be released from the oath, he told me about Alice. She'd taken an unknown horse—gray, by the way—to a show and won. It must have been a wonderful time. Because the horse was unknown and caused such a stir they came up with "keep 'em guessing." He wanted to go out in the same way down to the last detail. A smile, Terri, I looked at the picture and I saw your smile."

A gasp escaped her lips.

"I figured it'd all be over in a few hours. I could wait. If I'd told you Alfred wanted to see a winner's smile, a smile like Alice's . . . well, you didn't need anymore pressure."

Her face twisted in anguish. "But . . . but you ran off. You could've said good-bye."

"Lord knows I wanted to, but you were surrounded. Recently I'd hired Tony Eakin, a partner, so to speak, so I could take some time off from the clinic. Have a life. Hauling Green Luck was my first vacation in ten years." He chuckled. "I guess I acted like a kid out of school."

*Act* struck a chord. "You digress. Why did you leave?"

"Tony called right after you'd cleared the wall, told me Old Man Coleman's horse had a fractured cannon bone. Tony could've handled it."

He took a long drink of soda.

Terri held her breath.

"Except for one thing," he continued on a soft note. "Old Man Coleman, my first client. Actually"—he shrugged, gave a sigh—"he's not old. He was born that way. He thinks I'm the only one who can treat his stud horse. His wife was worried about his heart. I didn't want his demise on my conscience so I took off. When I got there Tony was handling Coleman's panic attack and the horse on his own"—he paused— "more or less."

He took a deep breath. "If you want to know the truth, it's not been easy for me to delegate the work-load. I'd handled it alone for too long. I had to be in control. I've passed that point now." He paused, his voice deepened. "You've shown me there's life be-yond the clinic."

He was so contrite, so repentant, she found herself searching for the right words. Her pulse raced. Awk-wardly she cleared her throat. "The truth isn't always so simple, is it?"

Drawing her close to him, he whispered in her ear. "No. No, it's not."

She shot upright. "But what about the research? That was down . . . downright . . . sneaky. You used me. That's what you did. You used me."

"That's what I wanted to show you."

He dragged the briefcase onto his lap. Shuffling through the Terri Page folder, he found the last page and handed it to her.

One glance at the date and she thought Albuquerque. In Robert's bold handwriting, "Research aborted. Too much in love with subject to be objective" jumped out at her.

Astonishment touched her pale face. His silvery-gray eyes caught hers. The tenderness of his expression did it.

Reeling, she was in his arms. He kissed her throat, her eyes. His lips traveled her face until he found her mouth.

Content, she murmured against his chest, "Now that I know the truth I understand where you were coming from."

The devilish grin was back. "Since I'm having true confessions there's something else you should know."

"Inquiring minds"—snuggling as close as she dared—"want to know."

"I have a son."

Speechless, her eyes widened. She backed away from him.

"Not only a son, but a son with a problem."

He hit a soft spot. "What kind of problem? Can I help?"

"I don't know if he can be helped. He's a bra snatcher."

She froze half a second. "Green Luck!" she squealed.

She dove back in his arms.

"After I finished at the clinic, I drove back to Fiddle. You'd left, but Alfred and I had a long talk. I told him how I felt about you. He insisted on giving me Green Luck on the condition I keep him for life. He wants to visit and watch"—he drew her closer—"Alice ride. I know, it was a slip, he meant you. Afterward, I cut for Fresno on a red-eye."

She could hardly speak. "Oh, Robert, I . . . don't know what to say."

"There's more."

She held her breath.

"I have another son."

Not knowing what to expect, she tensed.

"This one has a problem, too, but it can be fixed. He's scheduled for hind leg surgery."

"Festus! What is this? A ready-made family?"

He nodded. "It's a start."

Her hands trembled. Tears gathered. "I . . . I better ask. Any more revelations?"

"No"—nibbling her ear—"unless you want to count Mecate."

"Mecate?"

"My cat," he breathed on her throat.

Overwhelmed by the emotions swirling within, she struggled to make a final point. "I think you better take an oath vowing no more secrets."

The suggestion was all it took. Robert Daniel Bromwell DVM stiffened, licked his palms, slicked back his hair, executed operatic scales, and placed his hand over his heart.

"I hereby swear before the joy of my life that I will tell the truth, the whole truth and nothing but the truth as long as we both shall live. Can you forgive me?"

Laughter, mixed with happy tears, she returned to his arms. Her kiss and lingering embrace gave him his answer.